FIGHTING FOR ESME

BROTHERHOOD PROTECTORS WORLD

TEAM FALCO
BOOK ONE

JEN TALTY

BROTHERHOOD PROTECTORS

ORIGINAL SERIES BY ELLE JAMES

Brotherhood Protectors Yellowstone

Saving Kyla (#1)

Saving Chelsea (#2)

Saving Amanda (#3)

Saving Liliana (#4)

Saving Breely (#5)

Saving Savvie (#6)

Brotherhood Protectors Colorado

SEAL Salvation (#1)

Rocky Mountain Rescue (#2)

Ranger Redemption (#3)

Tactical Takeover (#4)

Colorado Conspiracy (#5)

Rocky Mountain Madness (#6)

Free Fall (#7)

Colorado Cold Case (#8)

Fool's Folly (#9)

Brotherhood Protectors Series

Montana SEAL (#1)

Bride Protector SEAL (#2)

BROTHERHOOD PROTECTORS WORLD

ORIGINAL SERIES BY ELLE JAMES

Brotherhood Protectors Yellowstone World

Team Wolf

Guarding Harper - Desiree Holt

Guarding Hannah - Delilah Devlin

Guarding Eris - Reina Torres

Guarding Payton - Jen Talty

Guarding Leah - Regan Black

FIGHTING FOR ESME

TEAM FALCO BOOK 1

USA Today Bestselling Author
JEN TALTY

A NOTE FROM JEN TALTY

I'd first like to thank Leanne Tyler, Stacey Wilk, Deanna L. Rowley, and Kris Norris for daring to jump into the fire with me. These four women are incredibly talented, and I'm honored to be working with them on this amazing project. I'd also like to thank Elle James for opening her spectacular world and letting us play in it.

One of my favorite things to do is work with other writers on projects like this. Being an author can be lonely. We spend hours at our desks with people who don't exist. So, plotting and sharing characters with a group is exciting, and when I find a group that is as awesome as this one, I can't wait to do it all again.

The five of us enjoyed creating five brothers with a unique set of circumstances and sharing their history in each of our books. After you read mine, please, continue with the rest of the series and enjoy each

Falco brother as they overcome the pains of the past and find hope in a new future.

You can learn more about Sparrow and Stone and their story by reading *Defending Sparrow*. And to find out about Clint and Avery's romance, check out *Defending Avery* by Regan Black.

Happy reading!

To all firefighters, especially those who came to my home one spring day in 1998 when my home was struck by lightning. Thank you for your dedication, your selflessness, and your bravery.

CHAPTER 1

TROY FALCO TOOK a handful of dry dirt and dropped it over the casket. The chunks of earth hit the wood like large rain pellets hurling from the heavens. He glanced over his shoulder at his four brothers and choked on the thick emotion that bubbled up from his gut.

He'd spent a lifetime fighting for this moment.

Trent, his twin, gave him a nod as he shifted his stance as if to tell him he'd done all the right things over the years. That all the sacrifice and all the pain each of them had endured had been worth it because it brought them to this juncture. Trent had regularly reminded Troy that he had been the one constant through all the ups and downs and years of the Falco brothers not being a cohesive unit, and how each one of them appreciated Troy's battles.

Today, despite their father, they were finally a family.

It amazed Troy what he could pull from a shake of the head. While he couldn't read his twin's thoughts, he knew how Trent's brain worked and what was in his heart and soul. He felt it deep in his core. He couldn't describe how the emotions came to him, or how each of his brothers' feelings touched him deeply, but no matter where in the world they were, the Falco boys were always connected. Not even their father could break that bond.

A big puffy white cloud floated across the bright blue sky, casting a giant shadow over only the gravesite.

That summed up the story of his father's existence.

Shawn Falco lived a complicated personal life, and he'd been estranged from his five boys for different reasons since each one had been old enough to make their own decisions.

However, he'd been a well-respected firefighter. Shawn might not have shown up for his children, but he did for the community, and now men and women from all over Colorado paid their respects. Troy and his brothers didn't know half the people who had stood in the distance with their somber expressions, nor did they understand the accolades they had given their father at the memorial service.

Seth, the oldest sibling, scoffed through most of it,

especially when a female firefighter named Kora gave a heartfelt speech. It had even more meaning considering she'd been injured in the line of duty yesterday, and she still managed to make it to Shawn's funeral. If a man could breathe fire, that's exactly what Seth had done. Troy had been concerned Seth would walk out or create a scene. But to his credit, Seth did neither.

However, he didn't have a single positive thing to say about their father or Kora.

Troy couldn't blame Seth. Shawn hadn't made it easy for any of them to be his son. Shawn had failed his first wife when he cheated. He failed his children daily, and Seth resented him to this day.

For the five Falco brothers, the current event wasn't about what anyone thought of their old man or even their feelings or opinions about the man they called dad.

While they laid their father to rest today, they also embarked on a new chapter. Troy had been dreaming about this since Marcus, the youngest of the Falco boys, left home to become a firefighter in the Marines.

How ironic that everyone at the funeral believed Troy and his brothers had honored their dad by following in *his* footsteps when they all had become firefighters. However, Troy, Trent, and Seth hadn't done so because it was what their father had been.

But because their mother had died in one.

Heath had been the product of an affair, and he'd once confided in Troy that he, in part, had become a firefighter because he wanted a connection to the man who had created him. More importantly, Heath wanted to know his brothers. To have a bond with them. Troy had always tried to keep the lines of communication with Heath open.

That hadn't worked out too well when they'd been teenagers. Something that Troy had been determined to change.

Marcus, the baby, was the only son from Shawn's second marriage, and for him, the reason was simple.

It was in his blood. He was a Falco. It wasn't about Shawn, but about the brothers who helped raise him. He'd talked about being a firefighter since Seth had left home and gave him all his fire trucks. Following in his four older brothers' paths had been a straightforward decision.

"It's hotter than blazes out," Seth, the oldest brother, said as he aggressively tossed his pile of earth into the grave, missing the casket altogether.

That caught a heartfelt chuckle from Trent, who quickly cleared his throat.

"And it's only May. If this heat continues with no rain, we'll have a ton of wildfires breaking out." Heath peered over the opening in the ground. He took hold of Seth's arm. "Anyone else waiting for him to jump out of that box and yell *do-over*?"

Trent burst out laughing before pounding his chest and covering his mouth, pretending to cough. "If I had a dollar for every time he tried to get a do-over for missing something important, like parent-teacher conferences, I'd be a rich man."

Seth laughed. "Last time I talked to the old man, he told me that everyone should be granted a few do-overs and I owed him a couple. Now that's fucking rich."

"How the hell do you have a do-over as a father?" Trent asked. "He always cared more about work than he did us."

"At least he cared enough about all of you to keep you." Heath took his shades from atop his head and placed them over his eyes. "But he did say taking me in at sixteen was his *do-over* with me and I better not screw it up."

"You all make him out to be the worst man in the world." Marcus, the baby, took two fistfuls of dirt and gently sprinkled them over the grave as if he were tossing precious jewels on the casket. "He wasn't that bad."

"He was an asshole," Heath said. "You just had the twins to help shelter you from all the bullshit. Especially Troy who stayed until he couldn't."

"Troy has always been like a nasty rash that wouldn't go away," Seth said with a hearty dose of sarcasm. "And I heard you were the asshole." Seth slapped Heath on the back. "I'm almost sorry I missed some of that."

"Health was one giant dick back then." Troy glanced one last time over his shoulder. In the last couple of months, he saw a side of his father he wished he hadn't.

Weak. Sad. Almost pathetic.

And dependent on Troy for everything.

Cancer had really kicked his ass and changed who Shawn was; however, it couldn't erase the past. "But Dad was a bigger one." Troy couldn't deny that on some level he loved his father. Respected him as a fellow firefighter. However, he didn't like him one bit. His father's priorities had been working and women. Not family, and he certainly didn't teach his boys how to be one.

No. He did his best to pit them against each other.

Each of Troy's brothers had left home the moment they turned eighteen, except Troy, and for the most part, they didn't look back. Troy had individual relationships with each of his brothers. He called, texted, and visited them regularly. He tried to get everyone together; however, that never worked out.

For years, Heath and Seth didn't even know each other, much less have a conversation.

And Marcus barely spoke to anyone but the twins.

Troy had served as the linchpin in the family. He was grateful for the relationships he had cultivated, but what he wanted was for him and his brothers to be a unit.

A team.

A family without the poison that was their father.

He glanced to his left, where Seth and Heath strolled down the hill, away from their father's grave.

Together.

Marcus and Trent flanked his left side.

Tears burned his scratchy eyes for the first time since he'd called hospice in the last hours of his father's life.

Troy had tried a few different times to get his brothers together.

But something always came up.

That all changed six months ago when the old man got sick, and Troy pleaded with his brothers to reunite. Not for the sake of Shawn Falco.

But for themselves.

Much to his surprise, he didn't have to twist anyone's arm. They all agreed. They each had to wrap up some loose ends in their lives, but not one of Troy's brothers said no to relocating and started new careers.

When Troy had called, Seth had already been looking for a place to plant roots in Fool's Gold.

It was fate.

"Hey, Troy. Who's that standing next to our vehicle?" Marcus asked.

Troy lifted his shades and squinted. "That's Hank

Patterson and Jake Cogburn. Our new bosses." Troy had taken the meetings with Hank and Jake while he looked after their father, so the rest of the brothers had yet to meet the bigwigs, except Seth, who had spent some time in Fool's Gold purchasing their new home.

"What are they doing here?" Seth asked. "I thought we were being briefed next week after we got settled at Paradise Ranch."

"Why do you keep calling it that?" Trent asked. "From the pictures I've seen, the house on that place we bought is run down. So is the bunkhouse. The barn. And every other building on that piece of land. We should call it the Money Pit."

"That's why we got it so cheap," Seth said.

"I think Paradise Ranch is perfect." Marcus always had a habit of being a glass-half-full kind of man. It came in handy sometimes, but other times it could be annoying. "Besides, we'll fix it up real nice."

"I call the barn," Trent said. "It looked rustic and my style."

"You don't have a style." Troy smiled. If anyone looked his way, they would have thought it utterly inappropriate considering the circumstances.

He didn't give a fuck.

"I take offense to that comment." Trent laughed. "I think you should live in the stables with a bunch of stinky horses just for saying that."

"I'm down with that and for the record, I love

horses." Troy slowed his pace. If the head of the Brotherhood Protectors and the head of the Colorado division showed up at the very tail end of his father's funeral, it couldn't be good news.

"I know you do, but I can't imagine you'd want to live with them." Trent glanced in his direction.

"You know that other livestock is kept in a barn, right?" Seth asked. "Cows, chickens, and other animals kept at a ranch all take up residence where you plan to sleep."

"Nope. The barn will be a home for people and people only. If I'm camping, I sleep in a tent; the bears sleep outside the tent. Same will go for the barn," Trent said, lowering his voice as they got closer to the SUV where Hank and Jake stood.

Troy adjusted his suit coat and stopped short of the vehicle. "Hank. Jake."

Hank stretched out his arm. "We're sorry for your loss."

"Thank you." Troy took Hank's hand in a firm shake.

"We apologize for interrupting your father's funeral," Jake said. "But it's important."

"No worries," Troy said. "What can we do for you?"

"We have a situation that we need Team Falco for and we honestly need you as soon as possible. Tomorrow if you can make it happen." Jake shifted his stance and leaned against the vehicle.

"Nothing is keeping us here," Seth said.

"We can be in Fool's Gold by morning," Marcus added. "Or even tonight if necessary."

"What's the situation?" Trent asked.

Troy puffed out his chest. This was precisely what he'd been dreaming about all these years.

He and his brothers.

Together.

All five of them huddled up next to each other as if they were a football team. A dose of adrenaline snaked through Troy's veins.

"It's twofold," Hank said. "First, we need all of you to fill in at the Fool's Gold Fire Station."

"There was a three-alarm fire that unfortunately injured eight firefighters in that house alone," Jake said. "They need the human resources and they need it now. The entire district is strapped thin."

"We're happy to saddle up and work," Seth said.

"It goes deeper than taking a few shifts," Jake said. "The fire claimed one life. Henri Jade, the fire chief. The investigator is working with the local sheriff's office, specifically, Sparrow Bishop."

"Did she take Stone's last name?" Hank asked. "Or did she keep Oakley?"

"Does it matter?" Jake shook his head. "She's married to one of our guys. Anyway, this fire has the sheriff's office and the investigator's hackles up."

"With loss of life—especially a fire chief—I'm sure the investigator won't leave any stone unturned."

Hank and Jake exchanged glances. "It's personal for this investigator."

"Why?" Marcus asked.

"The investigator is Esme Jade, Henri's daughter." Jake arched a brow.

"The state's going to let her stay on the case?" Troy asked. During his Air Force career, Troy worked closely with local fire departments. He saw many families who worked together. Fathers. Sons. Married couples. It was a thing in the world of fire-fighting, which made tragedies even more personal. There was a time when he knew deep in his soul that Trent had been hurt in a mission. He felt it in his bones. It was like someone had reached inside his body and twisted around his insides. He'd learned as a kid not to ignore that feeling.

Troy liked facts. He trusted facts. If he couldn't touch it, taste it, or see it, it didn't exist.

But when it came to family, he always listened to his gut. That wasn't an emotional thing; it was a pure connection he had with family that he didn't have with anyone else. It was stronger with Trent. Twin powers, they called it. However, he had it with Marcus and the more time he spent with Heath and Seth, the more he realized he'd always had it with them as well.

Now that he had all his brothers in one place, he didn't know what he'd do if he ever lost one. They were the fabric that made up who he was as a man.

"First, she's one of the best fire and arson investigators in the State of Colorado," Jake said. "Second, the fire hasn't been ruled arson, but if that is the case, Esme knows how to compartmentalize."

"How do you know that?" Heath asked. Interesting question coming from the man who preferred inanimate objects over breathing ones.

"Her mother was the Colorado Springs Firestarter," Jake said.

"You've got to be joking," Marcus said. "That woman set twenty fires and murdered twice as many people. But her name was Heather Roman. Not Jade."

"We recently watched a special about her on television," Trent said. "She's a religious nutjob. Honestly believed she was doing God's work. Cleaning the soul of Colorado, she was quoted as saying, or some such bullshit."

"Her lawyers tried to get her an insanity deal," Hank said.

"That was thirty years ago," Trent said. "How does the fire chief have an ex-wife that was a—"

"Henri adopted Esme when she was two years old," Hank said. "After he saved her from a burning building that her mother set fire to and left her to die because she believed the devil possessed Esme and God commanded it."

"Jesus," Troy muttered. "That's fucked up." Worse than anything his old man dished out. He exchanged a quick glance between Seth and Trent. Their mother had died in a fire. Seth had been seven years old, and he dragged Trent and Troy from that fire at the begging of their mother.

She didn't make it.

She told them she would be right behind them after she went to get Grandpa. Neither one made it out.

But worse, their father somehow blamed all of them for the death of his wife and father.

"Henri has protected Esme from her crazy mother for years. He was her father and he loved her. Esme is desperate to find out what happened."

"Desperation doesn't equate to the ability to compartmentalize," Seth said.

"We all want the same answers," Jake said. "The fire happened at seven last night and there is absolutely no reason why Henri would have been in that building alone in the first place. Esme will begin her investigation today."

"Any chance her mother could have orchestrated this from prison?" Heath asked.

"It's being looked into," Hank said. "But Heather had a particular pattern she followed. She never wavered. Every fire she set was to a shelter that helped prostitutes, or churches known for their missions to help the homeless, including sex-workers, except the first one that killed Esme's biological father. But we're shifting from the reason for our visit and why we need you in Fool's Gold ASAP."

"We can hit the road in the next hour," Seth said. "Troy and I have moved some things to our ranch, and the rest will come later. It's not a problem. Just tell us what shifts, and if we can work as a team, that would be great."

"You absolutely will work as a team of four," Jake said.

"There are five of us." Troy held up his hand and wiggled his fingers. "We all have unique skill sets, but all are capable of basic firefighting, and the entire point of us coming was to be a team both with the Brotherhood Protectors and with the station."

"And we're going to be honoring that contract. But the county is without a fire chief," Hank said. "Troy, we know you have some experience as a chief in the Air Force. While your four brothers are working at the Fool's Gold Fire Station, doing some investigative work, we want you to become the acting fire chief. This will give you access to everything. You can work with Esme, while keeping her safe, just in case this wasn't an accident, and keep her in check."

"It sounds like you believe this was no accident and that the chief was murdered." Troy had worn a few different hats during his career. He got his start right after he graduated from high school. His father had wanted him to work in his firehouse, but that would never happen. Two years later, Troy left his life behind after being left at the altar and followed his twin into the Air Force, where he became a Fire Protection Specialist—specifically, a fire investigator. From there, he left that role to become a captain and finally a chief before he left the military.

"We don't know. The fire is too fresh and under investigation. That's why we want Team Falco in charge. We have complete faith in you and your brothers," Jake said. "But we will want you to name a captain. And we want you to use all your skills. Not just basic firefighting. Henri wasn't always the most popular fire chief. Esme has her conspiracy theories, though again, she's good at compartmentalizing."

"Are you concerned she'll go rogue?" Heath asked.

"No. Not really. I'm more concerned that she's onto something and she'll get herself into trouble. She tends to be a bit of a lone wolf," Jake said. "That's why we want someone working with her from our team. And then you can control your team from the top down."

"Makes sense. I'd want Seth as captain," Troy said without batting an eyelash. He was the logical choice in this situation. Seth had the most experience and had been a captain before.

Heath scoffed, but it was more of a snicker.

Trent rolled his eyes, but cracked a smile, and Marcus kicked the ground, but again, did so with his lips turned upward.

"And you have the full backing of the Brotherhood Protectors. However, for this first assignment, no one will know that you are working for us except Sparrow," Hank said. "She'll be your point of contact regarding law enforcement."

"I'll send you a file with all the information and Esme will brief you sometime tomorrow," Jake said. "We can set up a time later for all of us to meet. Perhaps at the ranch."

"Sounds like a plan," Heath said.

"We'll see you tomorrow." Hank pulled open the vehicle door. "Again, we're sorry for your loss."

Jake limped around the hood. The engine roared to life.

Troy stepped back as the SUV rolled down the narrow street that curved through the cemetery. "I guess we better get our go bags and get to work."

For the first time in Troy's life, he had all his brothers at his side and it wasn't a fleeting moment.

Team Falco was a reality. They would work and live together for the first time since—well, ever.

Troy's heart lifted.

He glanced over his shoulder and mentally said one last goodbye to his father. As much as he didn't like the old man, he was grateful that Shawn Falco had given him four exceptional brothers.

CHAPTER 2

Esme Henri ducked her head under the yellow tape. The smell of charred wood mixed with death filled her nostrils. It was a unique scent that she wouldn't dare try to describe to a soul. A thick lump stuck in her throat. Every time she tried to swallow, it jumped right back, making it difficult to breathe. It was like a frog leaping across the yard, except it was lurching around her digestive system.

"Esme. What are you doing here?" Jim, the sheriff, asked. He strolled in front of what was left of the condemned building. The roof had caved, crushing the second floor into the first. The appliances stood proud, as did a few random walls, but everything else was unrecognizable.

Her heart dropped to her big toe. It was heavy and beat slowly. Her lungs burned with every breath.

JEN TALTY

"Trying to find out what started this fire." She waved her hand. "Or who started it."

"You were just at the morgue," Jim said softly as he rubbed the back of his neck. "Identifying your father's body. For your own mental health, you shouldn't be here. Take some time off. Rest and give yourself time to process and grieve. Let Colby handle all this."

She was so tired of people telling her what she should do and how she should do it. As if there were a checklist on how to properly deal with the sudden death of a parent. Her mind returned to why her father had been in this building in the first place. "This is my job." She squared her shoulders, drawing on her father's strength and support that he'd given her throughout her entire life. "I am the senior agent," she said.

George, her boss, hadn't been thrilled with her taking the lead. However, after an hour-long discussion, he'd agreed as long as she remained professional and kept him and Colby Knott, another fire and arson investor, in the loop, specifically, her right-hand man. She could handle that. Colby was a good investigator and she liked working with him when she could control the situation.

However, George hired the Brotherhood Protectors. Some new specialized team with firefighting experience. Some would be working in the fire

18

station and one would be stepping in as acting fire chief.

And her shadow.

Now that pissed her off for a variety of reasons.

She understood this wasn't because the victim had been her father.

It was because the chief had died in a fire.

She could get on board with hiring someone from a different county or even out of state as fire chief until the investigation was complete. But having this man be up in her business and the idea that she would have to report to him and work side by side with him made her want to jump right out of her skin.

"You don't have to do this." Jim placed his hand on her shoulder and squeezed gently. "It's okay if you want to pause and take a breath. I've assigned Sparrow to this and she'll keep you in the loop while you take some time to take care of yourself."

"Jim. I appreciate what you're saying, but I can't sit around and do nothing. I need to be active in finding out why my father was in the building and how the fire started in the first place."

"I can understand that," he said. "Have you heard that the new fire chief is being announced at the top of the hour?"

"I sure have. I don't know if I'm insulted by this personal bodyguard thing or feel like everyone has my back."

"Don't take it personally," Jim said.

"Easier said than done." She glanced at her watch. "I'll have to set a timer. I want to watch the announcement."

"Shit," Jim mumbled. "It's being done here."

"You've got to be kidding me." She sucked in a deep breath, then exhaled. Loudly. "Why wasn't I informed of that juicy piece of information?"

"That I can't answer, but at least you'll get to meet Troy Falco."

"Falco? That's his name. As in one of Shawn Falco's sons?"

"You've met him?" Jim asked.

"I haven't met any of Shawn's boys and I've only had the privilege, though I wouldn't call it that, of meeting Shawn three or four times. Not my favorite human being, but he was a well-respected firefighter."

"That he was."

"Didn't he die? Like days ago?" she asked, doing her best to pull up her mental checklist, focusing on her job.

"The funeral was yesterday," Jim said. "They are, however, eager to start work."

"Didn't a few from the Fool's Gold station attend the funeral?"

"As many that could go, did," Jim said. "Shawn Falco was an interesting character. You either loved him or hated him. But professionally, everyone had to respect him as he did a lot for his community."

"How did his children feel about him?"

Jim arched a brow. "That's relevant, why?"

"It's not. But you've got me all curious now." She cocked her head and gave the sheriff her best sarcastic smile.

He laughed. "I suspect they have resented the hell out of their dad. I would have if Shawn Falco had been my old man." Jim rested his hand on her shoulder. "From what both Hank and Jake have told me about the Falco boys, this town is in good hands with Troy at the helm."

The Brotherhood Protectors organization brought in the best of the best. The true elite. She shouldn't doubt the kind of man who would be taking her father's place, even if it was only temporary. This Troy Falco would be working not only as a firefighter for the State of Colorado, but he was an agent for Hank Patterson.

That meant something.

Esme pointed to Sparrow, huddled around the side of the burnt building with an off-duty firefighter.

Billy Rocha.

She squared her shoulders. "Have we heard how Micky Glass is doing?" Even though she no longer worked as a firefighter nor lived in Fool's Gold, she still knew everyone in her old station.

"He's having surgery this morning where they will be plating five of his ribs," Jim said. "He'll be on a ventilator for at least three or four days. He's in bad shape."

"That sucks," she said. "I'm going to see what Billy and Sparrow are discussing."

Jim nodded. "Sparrow is your point of contact, but you know how to reach me if you need anything."

"Thank you." She tucked her hair behind her ears, a habit that drove her father crazy. She blew out a puff of air and made her way toward Sparrow. A burning sensation filled the center of her chest.

Her mother had already tried reaching out to her from prison. God only knew what that woman wanted to say and sadly Esme was tempted to find out.

"Esme," Sparrow said, glancing up from her notepad. "I'm so sorry about your father."

"I am too." Billy squeezed her biceps. "I want you to know I tried to find him, but the smoke was too thick. I don't know how Micky got up the stairs. It was hotter than balls inside." He wiped his face. Dark circles hung from his eyes. Behind them she thought she saw a world of pain.

But with Billy, she could never be sure. He was the kind of man you had to trust at work, and he always pulled through during an emergency. However, he was never the first choice to go racing into a burning building with. His arrogance always rubbed people the wrong way.

"I called for Henri. Over and over again. But he didn't answer. When I lost Micky in the smoke, that's when the fire got out of control and I knew I had to get out." Billy wore a fresh shirt and jeans, but the smell of burnt wood still clung to his skin like an old glove.

"I feel terrible about what happened to Micky." Esme appreciated his candor. She knew it couldn't be easy for him. Being a firefighter didn't come without risk, but no one ever expected it to happen while off duty. "And I hate to make you keep reliving the experience, but I need an official statement."

"I was asking Sparrow if I could give it a little later. Micky is in surgery right now and I promised his wife I'd be there when he came out."

His ex-wife, but Esme didn't think she should be correcting Billy. His buddy was fighting for his life and could use all the support he could get.

"Maybe I could give it to you both at the same time. The station is stretched for manpower and I'm going to be pulling double shifts," Billy said.

"I'm sorry, but I didn't realize my father had decided on your case." Esme bit down on her tongue. This wasn't the time or place to bring up the fact that Billy was not only off duty, but that he'd been suspended for insubordination and consistent refusal to follow protocol on and off the job.

Rushing into the burning building that took her father's life was considered dangerous and one of the reasons Billy had been suspended. It broke protocol and the new chief might consider tacking that on his punishment.

But she wasn't going to have that discussion. She wasn't his superior. She was the investigator, making an enemy of him wouldn't do her any favors. She needed facts. She needed to know every detail of what he'd seen. Of how that fire had behaved. No stone could go uncovered. For now, she'd play nice in the sandbox.

Billy furrowed his brow. "He didn't. But I expect to plead my case to the new acting fire chief this afternoon. The Fool's Gold station house is down at least eight firefighters for who knows how long. Keeping me sidelined isn't doing our community any good."

"Have you been in contact with the new chief?" Esme asked.

"I heard he arrives today and I've requested his ear," Billy said. "Now, how about we do these interviews first thing in the morning?"

"That works for me." Esme nodded.

"Oh. I'm sorry. I've got meetings. Can you come by the sheriff's station after you're done with Esme? I should be free around eleven." Sparrow shrugged.

"Shit. That's going to eat up my entire morning." Billy exhaled. "I'll make it work."

"Thanks. I appreciate it." Sparrow tucked her notepad into her pocket.

"Esme, text me where to meet you," Billy said.

"Will do." Esme nodded.

Billy pulled a baseball cap from the back of his jeans, pulled it over the top of his head, and headed across the street.

Esme surveyed the scene while she waited for him to disappear out of sight.

"I can't believe you dated him." Sparrow's words smacked Esme right between the eyes.

In high school, Billy Rocha was the most popular guy on campus. He was handsome, smart, and going places. She considered his cocky attitude charming. But what did she know, especially when her own father could be a tad on the arrogant side. It wasn't until the end of their relationship that she understood there was a vast difference between confidence —her father—and believing that your own shit didn't stink—Billy.

She hadn't seen it until they both were working as firefighters.

"I was young and stupid."

"For three years?" Sparrow's question was more of a sarcastic remark and one that Esme had become accustomed to over the years. "I have never understood what you saw in him. Double-dating with you back then had to be the most painful experience I've ever had to go through."

"Somehow I think being Lilly's daughter would have been more difficult," Esme said. She and Sparrow had always sparred about their criminal mothers. Esme's was a pyromaniac-murdering bitch. And Sparrow's mom was once the leader of the biggest gang in Colorado. "Or maybe that guy Brett you dated. Talk about boring." Esme rolled her eyes. "That was painful to watch."

"Boring isn't the right word to describe him. He was so in love with himself it was disgusting." Sparrow laughed. "He married a model. He lives in LA with two kids and drives a BMW. He has even more money than his parents do. Although, I've heard rumors on how he came into his money might be a bit on the sketchy side."

"What do you mean?"

"Shady investments. Borderline con artist. Snake oil salesman kind of thing," Sparrow said. "My father always thought he was the kind of man who would toss his own mother under the bus to make a fast dollar, which is totally ironic coming from my dad."

"I heard through the grapevine that Brett was at the casino a couple of weeks ago," Esme said. "My dad never liked him. Thought he was fake, a wannabe socialite who could never play by that set of rules. He also didn't believe his account of what happened at the Smith's house the night of the fire. He never thought for one second that Andrew Kimber had anything to do with it, but there was no proof."

"Andrew had motive. Those girls were especially nasty to him."

"I know." Esme nodded. "I remember when they took Billy to the station to be questioned. He was so shaken up about Cathy's death."

"He cheated on you with her."

"He went out with her before me. It was the other way around." Although, there were rumors that he and Cathy would meet up late at night. Esme had no proof, and Billy emphatically denied it.

"Or maybe he had his cake and ate it too." Sparrow tilted her head. "I don't care that he changed after that fire, he was seeing both of you."

"Maybe, but that was a long time ago, and that fire really affected him." Esme understood that Billy's reckless attitude was in part because of the way in which Cathy had been trapped inside her bedroom with no way of escaping.

Billy didn't want that to ever happen to anyone else. He couldn't imagine how horrifying that had to have been for Cathy and he didn't want anyone else to ever experience that again. At least not on his watch.

"You know, I talked to your dad a couple of times about that fire. He always thought those boys were covering up something but couldn't figure out what or why. But he did say there was no evidence that any of those boys started that fire. That said, I never understood why your father put up with Billy when he didn't particularly care for him."

"As a man, my dad thought Billy was slime. He never trusted his intentions when it came to me. But he did respect him as a firefighter. It drove him batshit crazy that Billy constantly broke the rules. Bending them was one thing, but blatantly being disrespectful was something my father couldn't tolerate and he'd had it with Billy. If it wasn't for captain after captain going to bat for Billy, I bet my dad would have fired him a long time ago." During the years she dated Billy, her dad put up with the relationship because he loved his little girl. He figured it was a crush and would go away soon enough. He constantly told her that boys would come and go and to keep her heart open.

But it didn't. She and Billy had too much in common.

They both loved country music.

Both had an aptitude for English and loved to read the same kinds of books.

They both had been at the Smith house the night of the fire and that changed who they were to the core.

And they both wanted to be firefighters.

The only difference was that Esme excelled in the classroom and Billy was all brawn. He wanted to be a hero. To be revered in the eyes of the community. For him, it wasn't about *protect and serve*. He didn't want to only save people. He wanted to be honored for doing so.

She remembered the first time others were recognized and he'd been overlooked. The anger that filled his heart had been the straw that broke the camel's back. The entire crew had been praised, but two other firefighters had been called out for their heroism. While Billy had gone above and beyond, he'd also downright ignored orders. He'd pissed off their captain, who told her father, who in return chose other deserving first responders.

Billy spent an hour taking his anger out on a punching bag and then using his mouth to rant about all that he'd done to save the family. What he'd done in the line of duty. How deserving he was over the men who had received a medal. And how she should have stood up to her father, instead of agreeing with his assessment of Billy's lack of respect for the chain of command.

That had successfully ended their relationship.

He wasn't a horrible person for wanting the glory for a job that he got paid shit to do, and the hard part for Esme had been that Billy was damn good at his job, when he did it the right way. However, if she were being honest with herself when it came to the night of her father's death, she might have done the same thing if she'd been walking by and saw the fire chief's truck.

"Speaking of all things Billy," Sparrow said. "Do

you know if your dad would have reinstated him this time? My understanding was that he's been suspended so many times his termination could have been on the spot."

"He could have been canned the last time he was suspended, but that would have been stupid, considering the infraction itself was so minor."

"This time he was suspended for a month. That's a statement," Sparrow said.

"My father wanted Billy to feel the pain of his accumulated actions. And he wanted other firefighters to understand that protocols were there not to punish or make their jobs harder, but to save lives." Esme rolled her neck. As much as her dad had been frustrated with Billy, he sure as hell wasn't going to fire the man. Or at least she didn't think he was since his preoccupation had to do with other things.

She wasn't supposed to know about the crazy man communicating with her mother, but she did. Her dad wanted to protect her from that, and so far, all that had transpired was letter writing. Nothing more. Nothing less. But it was the tone of the correspondence that had her father in a tizzy. This had nothing to do with Billy, but maybe it somehow had something to do with her father's death.

"There's something I haven't told you," Esme said. "But it can't be here. Can you meet me at my dad's place tonight? I'm going to be staying there while this investigation is going on."

"That sounds ominous. Can you give me a hint?"

"It's something my dad was working on."

"Sure thing. Look." Sparrow pointed toward the south side of the building. "Here comes the new acting fire chief."

A man, approximately six feet tall with sandy-brown hair and a muscular build—not that any of that mattered—approached with George Armond.

The man she didn't know pulled a pair of shades from his face, exposing a set of eyes the color of the sky. He set his sunglass on top of his thick hair, which was a little longer than standard for a fire-fighter. Certainly longer than her father would have approved.

Not to mention the facial hair.

It wasn't a lot.

But firefighters weren't allowed to have anything but a mustache, which she generally hated.

"You can close your mouth and stop gawking," Sparrow whispered.

Esme blinked and snapped her lips together. "He's a tall drink of something, isn't he."

"Not half as sexy as my husband, but not bad." Sparrow laughed. "I hear he's got four brothers. All of them will be working undercover at the Fool's Gold Fire Station and one of them is his twin."

"I hope not identical," she said under her breath. Her system lit up like the grand finale of a fireworks show. It was rare that a man had this kind of effect on her body. Looks weren't what made her fall for a man, however. They might get her attention, but they weren't what held it. He needed to be innovative. Kind. Generous. Love the outdoors. Be able to laugh at himself, but have a serious side. But most importantly, he had to respect her independence.

She squared her shoulders and sucked in a deep breath, settling her nerves. "Hey, George," she said.

"How are you holding up?" He leaned in and kissed her cheek. He'd been overly affectionate in the last twenty-four hours, making her nuts. "He was a good man and we're all going to miss him."

"Thank you." A thick lump formed in the center of her throat.

"Sparrow." George nodded. "I'd like for both of you to meet Troy Falco. He'll be the new fire chief."

"It's a pleasure," Sparrow said. "I'll be your point of contact." She pulled out her cell and waved it. "Unfortunately, duty calls." She stepped away to answer her phone.

"I need to get back to the office," George said. "Troy. Don't hesitate to reach out if you need anything at all."

"Thanks. I appreciate it."

She watched as Troy gave George a firm handshake.

"I'm sorry for your loss," Troy said.

Snapping her gaze to his eyes, her lungs deflated. She tried sucking in a deep breath, but only gasped.

He conveyed a deep sense of understanding in his intense stare.

"I can only imagine how hard it is for you to be here today."

"I'm sure this isn't easy for you either, considering you just lost your dad as well."

"Did you know Shawn?" Troy asked.

"I'd met him a couple of times," she admitted. She'd honestly been shocked to find out he had five boys. He seldom talked about them. "My father knew him relatively well."

"While I never met your dad, I would gather it's safe to say he knew my father better than I did." Troy reached out, curling his long, thin fingers around her biceps. "I will do everything I can to find out what happened here. So will my brothers."

Her eyes stung with tears, but she did her best to rein them back in front of the new chief. Her father always told her there was a time and a place.

This was not it.

"I know your emotions are raw right now and I hate to have to jump right into this, but my press conference is in fifteen, so what can you tell me so far?"

"Absolutely nothing," she said. "Billy, one of the off-duty firefighters—"

"The one who's not hospitalized and who was suspended three weeks ago?" Troy asked.

"That's the one," she said. "He hasn't given his

statement yet. He just left to go see Micky who is having surgery."

"I heard all about that." Troy planted his hands on his hips and scanned the area. "Has he said anything about the fire or what happened inside?"

"Only that he and Micky got separated about the time the smoke got thick and the fire raged. I have spoken to a few firefighters who were first on the scene and they said the building went up like kindling."

"Anyone think the fire behaved erratically?"

"No one said that; however, Kora Garrison thought the color of the smoke was too dark and the fire ran too hot too fast from when it was called in."

"I'd like that timeline," Troy said. "I'd also like a list of every firefighter who was here and if possible, I want to be present for all interviews."

She cocked her head. She'd been a fire investigator for the last six years. Before that, she'd been a cop for five years after having her start as a firefighter for four years. In all her experiences, the fire chief never sat in on the investigators' interviews. Police officers did. The fire marshal did.

But not her dad.

"We allowed many firefighters to attend your father's funeral," Esme said. "I've asked them to return here today to walk through things with me, so I'm happy to let you join us."

"I understand that's not typical protocol and I

promise not to step on your toes. But it's one way to meet those under me, but my other bosses also have a bad feeling about this fire."

"And what does your gut say?"

"That it didn't like the breakfast sandwich I got at some gas station and I'm going to need to buy one of those special appliances so I can make my own."

She chuckled, enjoying his sense of humor. Her father would have appreciated it. "Not what I meant."

"When I was in the Air Force, I had your job for a couple of years. While I trust my instincts, they're useless if I don't have the facts to back them up. So, right now, whatever my gut is telling me, I'm filing until I have the necessary facts to back it up."

Shit. Her father would have loved this man.

"Did you ever let your instincts guide your investigation?"

"Is that a generic question? Or are you looking for advice from the fire chief?"

"Both," she admitted.

"I try very hard to keep my emotions from clouding my judgment and I've learned over the years that gut reactions are often led by the heart, not the mind." He arched a brow. "Now, I have a press conference to give. It will only take about fifteen minutes. I'm a man of few words."

"I doubt that."

He laughed. "In this case, I don't have much to say

and I don't plan to answer too many questions. So, please wait for me before interviewing anyone."

"I can do that."

"I've done a lot of things in my life, but standing in front of a bunch of reporters is not one of them." He rubbed his hands together and blew out a puff of air. "Do you have any words of wisdom for me?"

"My dad always said that less was more."

"That's good advice." Troy nodded.

"The only reporter out there worth talking to is Sally Wilber. The rest of them are bloodsucking sensationalist assholes."

"That's even better." He smiled. "I'll see you right back here in a few." He turned, stuffing his hands in his pockets, and strolled toward the front of the building.

Inwardly, she sighed as she tilted her head and watched him saunter away.

Damn. She lifted her chin and stared at a big puffy white cloud that floated across the sky. "Daddy, I can almost hear you whispering to go for it. But nope. I have to work with him." She closed her eyes and felt a warmth fill her body. It was as if her father wrapped his arms around her in a big bear hug, reminding her that certain distractions in life were a good thing and that she didn't have enough of them.

He hadn't been in a relationship since his wife died of breast cancer a little over a year ago. They'd been together since Esme had turned seven and he loved her with all his heart.

Companionship is important. One shouldn't go through life without it. That's what her father always used to tell her. He reminded her that when he took her in, he'd suffered great loss, and while she hadn't been a replacement, she did fill his heart with joy.

Becoming her father had been the experience of a lifetime and falling in love with Phoebe had been the second-greatest gift he'd ever been given.

She'd never been one to believe in the afterlife. She wasn't religious. But she did believe in connections, and she and her father had always had one. He'd always known when she'd been hurting or was scared. It didn't matter where in the world she was, he had this uncanny ability to be in tune with her emotions. In this moment, they were raw and she missed her father terribly.

Troy was eye candy.

His sense of humor was dry and exactly what she needed to help her through the investigation.

His sensitive eyes conveyed a deep understanding where others felt sorry for her.

It was as if her father sent him for more than to help her find answers.

CHAPTER 3

TROY PULLED into the Paradise Ranch with a truck full of gifts. He parked his vehicle in front of the main house. Marcus sat on the front steps with a frown and a beer. He didn't bother to get up. Troy remembered that expression, and he didn't like it.

"You look exactly like the day I drove off for the Air Force, but you weren't old enough to drink back then." Troy had never had so many mixed emotions as the day he left home. His heart had been crushed, and his father's words of wisdom had been, *I told you so.* Which was hilarious because his dad had actually liked Darlene. He'd told Troy she was a good catch and don't fuck up a good thing.

After Darlene had left him standing at the altar like a fool, Troy couldn't stand being in Denver. He hated leaving Marcus alone with their dad, but Marcus had been the one who pushed Troy into following his twin into the Air Force. Marcus held back the tears the day Troy drove off, but he couldn't have been prouder of his big brother.

The letters that came in the following weeks proved it. Marcus might have struggled being the only kid left, but he did what they all had done and held his head high.

"What's bothering you?" Troy asked.

"Seth." Marcus lifted his beer and took a hearty swig. He shook his head and sighed. "You have died and made him boss."

Troy chuckled. Because Troy was twenty minutes older than Trent, it put him as the third child of five.

The exact middle kid.

If you believed in the whole birth order thing, you would think Troy would be the wild and crazy one.

The one who broke the rules.

But that wasn't Troy. He had all the attributes of the oldest child.

"Seth is expecting us to have breakfast together. He even suggested a schedule. Like we're all going to sit around the table every morning, break bread, and sing 'Kumbaya' or some such bullshit. Since when have we ever done that?"

The only reason Seth wanted them to share a meal was because the man couldn't cook. It was almost comical. Troy had no idea why Seth didn't come out and say it, but he would enjoy poking fun at him and all his brothers. He'd waited a lifetime for these moments. He wasn't going to waste them.

"This is what put that sourpuss look on your face?" Troy leaned against the hood of his car and folded his arms. Something else had gotten under his little brother's skin.

"I heard some chatter at the fire station today about Henri Jade." Marcus squared his shoulders and held Troy's gaze. "Specifically that he'd been acting paranoid lately."

"About?"

"I didn't get much," Marcus said. "I wasn't part of the conversation and they weren't too keen on continuing the gossip, but I found out that Henri had interviewed everyone regarding Billy Rocha and Micky Glass."

"They're the two firefighters who happened to be headed to The Bottom of the Barrel Tavern and saw the building on fire. Micky's fighting for his life."

Marcus nodded.

"They were both suspended for insubordination and were up for review. I haven't had a chance to read their files, so I don't know much about them, other than they are cocky. But from the few firefighters I've talked with, they seem well liked and respected."

"They are, which is why the men and women in the station house thought it strange when Henri started asking different questions that had nothing to do with the incident that got them suspended, specifically about Billy and past infractions."

"Which ones?" Troy asked.

"Everyone stopped talking when I came into the room, so I didn't get details," Marcus said. "It will take some time for anyone with the last name Falco to get those firefighters to trust them on that level."

Troy rubbed the back of his neck. "Billy wanted to meet with me today. I rescheduled it for the end of the week. I told him I needed time to settle into my new job and review his file. He wasn't happy with that and reminded me of how thin the firehouse was with manpower."

"The schedule will be grueling," Marcus said. "But we've got it covered."

"Make sure Seth lets me know if you need more human resources and keep your eyes and ears open. Maybe it's nothing, but there was absolutely no reason for Henri to be in that building, especially alone."

"Will do."

"And as far as breakfast goes. Enjoy it while it's just the five of us. One of these days, someone will fall in love, get married, and have a family."

That brought out a chuckle and a smile from his kid brother. "Like anyone would have any of us. Being Shawn Falco's boys makes us damaged goods regarding women."

"That's not entirely true." However, it wasn't a false statement either.

Shawn Falco had a charming personality. Women tended to fall at his feet, and he was never without a girlfriend.

A bone of contention with Troy and all his brothers. Not because they didn't want their father to be happy, but because their dad didn't show up for them when it mattered.

Like when Heath landed at their doorstep when he was sixteen and needed more than biology.

"Maybe not." Marcus smiled. "By the way. You're on cooking duty tomorrow morning and I want your famous French toast bake. I haven't had that since you left."

Troy inwardly groaned. That had been Darlene's recipe and the last time he'd made it had been two days before she became a runaway bride. That had been the last time he'd eaten any form of the breakfast meal. He'd never told his brothers, although Trent had an idea.

He and Trent had that twin thing going on.

"Anything for you, baby brother," Troy said.

"I'm a grown-ass man. Stop calling me that."

"Okay. Kid."

Marcus rolled his eyes with a whopper of a smile on his face.

"Do me a favor and go get everyone else, and while you're at it, snag me a beer," Troy said.

Marcus jumped to his feet and took off inside the house, which Seth had claimed for himself. Only fitting since Seth had found the property in the first place. Besides, Troy had developed a distaste for all things homey, thanks to his ex-fiancée and the house they had purchased—in his name only—leaving him with a mortgage he couldn't afford. He took a loss on that place, and he'd admit his bitterness only to himself.

Troy strolled around to the back of his pickup. Each of his brothers had found a spot on the land that they could call their own. Marcus practically did a cartwheel when he found out there was a helicopter hangar with a place he could turn into a private apartment for himself because what five grown men wanted to live in a house together.

Heath took the bunkhouse. There was a whole bunch of irony wrapped up in that choice. While Heath wasn't antisocial or anything, he didn't necessarily enjoy people. The bunkhouse was set up to house a group of cowboys. It was improbable that Heath would ever have houseguests.

Troy reached inside the flatbed and unhooked the tailgate. He glanced to his right and stared at the barn which had become Trent's home. Inside a loft that Trent was making into nice sleeping quarters. Trent had the opposing personality to Troy. Yin and Yang, they were often called as kids. And it was true. There Troy was often quite serious, while Trent was telling jokes. His humor carried him through the hard times, where Troy clung to order and rules. Trent like to fly by the seat of his pants, and he did it well. Troy needed a plan. A road map.

But at the end of the day, Trent always understood Troy in a way that his other brothers didn't.

It was a twin thing.

Next to it was the stable, the building Troy had claimed. It was perfect for him not only because it already had sleeping quarters, but it had an office where Troy could set up security for the entire ranch, which he'd already started working on, but it would take a while before he'd have it to where he'd feel as though they were protected.

The sound of the front screen door slamming shut caught his attention. He peered over the side of his truck and smiled.

Team Falco.

Those two words would never get old.

"What the hell is this all about?" Heath grumbled, holding a slice of pizza in one hand and a soda in the other.

Marcus jogged down the steps and handed Troy a beer. Trent was one step behind him with an extra paper plate. Seth sauntered across the gravel and leaned against the hood of the car. Most people who met Seth often misunderstood him simply because he had the best resting bitch face of the family. "What's put that stupid grin on your face?"

"I've bought us all housewarming gifts." Troy felt like a kid in a candy store. It reminded him of when he'd been a small boy and his mom would take him to watch the Christmas tree lighting downtown. He didn't have too many memories of his mom, but he cherished the few he did have.

"Oh, this should be interesting." Heath stuffed the rest of his food into his mouth.

"Do you remember the last time he bought us all presents?" Trent asked. "He got me a *Ghostbusters* doll."

"That was classic." Seth slapped Trent on the back. "All right, little bro. Let's see what you got in the back of that truck."

Troy rubbed his hands together. His heart raced and his blood pumped through his system. He decided to start with the oldest and work his way down. That seemed to make the most sense. He pulled out a limited edition fire engine that he'd picked up at a gas station in town along with a T-Shirt.

"Oh, my God. I love it." Seth snagged the shirt and read the words on the front. "*I still play with fire trucks.* God. I remember giving them all to Marcus the day I left."

"I had to hide them because Dad wanted to throw them away. He kept calling you a traitor," Marcus said. "For two years I only played with them in my closet."

"That's hilarious." Seth tossed the shirt over his shoulder and held up the truck. "This is really cool. Thanks, bro."

"My pleasure." Troy snagged the next gift and handed it to Heath.

He held the Lincoln Logs fishing set up in the air and stared at it for a long moment before a big goofy smile came across his face. "When I first moved in with you all and Dad, you and Trent had this set. You used to tell me that it was the only way you'd ever be able to go fishing because Dad wouldn't take you."

"But you did," Trent said.

"Yeah, but I never had my own set of these." Heath blew out a puff of air. "Thanks."

Troy nodded as he moved on to his twin. Sometimes it wasn't fair how well they knew each other.

"No fucking way." Trent pulled the gift from Troy's hands before he even had it out of the truck. "A Ouija board. Man, you shouldn't have. I say we break out this bad boy and see if we can call on the old man's spirit."

"I'd say that's a hard no," Seth said.

"I'm with Seth on that one." Troy laughed. "All right, Marcus. Are you ready? Because this is good. For as long as you could talk, you've wanted this. You used to run around in your diaper begging for one."

"You couldn't have fit a pool in the back of your truck," Trent said.

"Oh, yes, I could and I did." Troy pulled out an

inflatable pool. "I figure this can be used until we figure out if and where we want a real pool."

"We could put fish in it and buy some real fishing poles while we call up some dead spirits," Trent said.

"And then my fire engine can use the water to fill up," Seth added. "I feel like I've been transported into my childhood, only it's an alternate universe."

"Yeah. One where it was a happy, normal one," Trent said.

"What did you get yourself?" Heath asked.

"Maybe he got himself a good-looking woman." Seth pointed to a white Jeep that rolled down the long gravel driveway.

"That's Esme Jade." Troy closed the tailgate to his truck and ran his fingers through his hair. The only people he expected to visit them at the ranch would have been someone from the Brotherhood Protectors. It wouldn't be a social call if Esme needed to see him in person.

"She's hot," Trent said.

"She's off-limits to any man with the last name Falco." Troy cleared his throat. That had come out way too territorial.

"Does that include you?" Heath poked his shoulder.

Inwardly, his answer was a resounding *no*. "Absolutely. We all have a job to do and that's to find out if the fire that killed her father was an accident or not."

"Actually, that's her job," Trent corrected. "We're here to support and protect."

After meeting Esme, Troy felt different about their first assignment with the Brotherhood Protectors. Something about this case stunk. The dots were so far apart that it was impossible to connect. He had no facts to support his gut instincts, which added to his frustration.

He tried to remind himself that he'd barely moved into his office, much less had a chance to review all the files or look at any of the reports that had come his way.

The interviews they conducted today painted a picture of two firefighters who often went against the grain.

One more than the other.

But they were good men and no one seemed to distrust them in the field. That was an essential piece of information. As a firefighter, if you didn't trust the man or woman running into that burning building, you might as well be dead. For Troy, that meant anything Billy or Micky had done, it wasn't something his coworkers wouldn't have considered doing under the same circumstances.

However, Troy was bothered by the number of times Billy had been suspended for insubordination, although he hadn't seen his file yet.

She parked her vehicle behind his and stepped out of the car.

"Hey, Esme," Troy said. "Meet all my brothers."

She waved. "I can see the family resemblance."

His brothers all grunted and waved.

"What brings you by?" he asked.

"Official business," she said.

He glanced over his shoulder. "They are included in the investigation. So, whatever you need to say, you can do so in front of them."

She nodded. "For starters, I have some files I found of my fathers that I thought you might want." She waved them. "I also have some information from the fire. I thought we could go over it. I would have called, but I didn't realize you were on my way to my dad's place."

"No worries." He took the files.

"Billy called me on my way here. He's not happy."

"I'm not making a decision on Billy yet." Troy didn't appreciate Billy trying to get to him through Esme.

"He'll have to get over it," Seth said. "We start our first shift in the morning. The station is in good hands."

"I'm sure it is." She glanced toward the sky. "I've been playing everything over in my head all day and there's one thing that doesn't sit right with me."

"What's that?" Troy asked.

"If I were walking by that building with a fellow firefighter, I would have gone in if I thought someone could be trapped. But I would never separate. Not without protective gear. Not without being in communication with someone on the outside. It would be suicide." She shifted her gaze back to Troy.

A world of pain lived behind her kind eyes. He felt it in his core, much like he could feel his siblings' emotions. He swallowed. He'd always had strong empathy associations with others, but never to this level. That had been reserved for his brothers. This threw him off his game, and he had to take a moment to collect his thoughts. He stole a quick glance at Trent so he could retain his composure.

"I've known Billy my entire life. He and I started out as firefighters together before I went off and became a police officer and then an investigator. He's a lot of things. But I've never known him to be that reckless."

"Protocols are in place for a reason," Heath said.

"Bending them is one thing, but a total disregard ends in a loss of life." Seth drove the point home with his words. "We all have different degrees in which we are willing to go rogue. Troy has always been the one who keeps us in check. He's like a mental moral compass for all of us, constantly reminding us of why there are rules."

"I'm the same way," she said. "However, when it comes to saving human lives, I think we can all agree, we'll go the extra mile."

Troy exchanged a glance between Trent and Seth.

Had Seth not listened to their mother, they might

be dead. But had their mom listened to Seth and gotten out of the house, she'd still be alive.

There might not have been any way to save Grandpa at that point.

But that was a lifetime ago.

"Are you asking me as the fire chief to reinstate Billy?" He arched a brow.

"God, no," she said. "It's how he and Micky got separated and the fact that Micky went all the way upstairs that I'm questioning."

"Who got Micky out of the building?" Troy asked.

"The first two firefighters inside were David Harris and Kyle Tagget. They went in the front, when Billy came running out the back at what appeared to be the same time. According to Billy, he fled before the floor caved in. David and Kyle entered right after and were able to carry Micky to safety. They tried to go back in, but it was too hot and dangerous."

"Where was your father found?" Marcus asked.

"In the living room," Esme said. "I don't have the structural report, but my walk around tells me the ceiling first collapsed above the dining room based on the fire pattern."

"How did Billy escape the house?" Trent asked. "You said he came running out the back. Does that mean the back door? Or something else?"

"Through a window in the family room," Esme said. "He ended up with ten stitches on his arm. A few more cuts and scrapes. Mild smoke inhalation. But that's about it."

"He's a lucky man," Heath said.

"Billy has nine lives." Esme tucked her blond hair behind her ears. "Part of the reason—I believe—he's so arrogant sometimes."

"Could be," Troy agreed. "Do you have any reason to believe that Billy could have set the fire?"

Esme's eyes grew wide. Her lips parted. "He's a lot of things, but no. I don't see him as an arsonist. He loves being a firefighter. It's all he's ever known."

"Firefighters becoming arsonists is a thing," Marcus said. "I've been reading about it."

"Well, I don't think that's what happened here, but I'm certainly willing to entertain the theory, if the evidence points me in that direction." Esme nodded.

"What about your mother?" Seth asked.

"That would be kind of hard considering she's in prison." Esme held up her hand. "Yes, I'm aware that there are men who write her and that she does have a bit of a cult following, but all her mail is checked and my father and I have always been informed if there's anything suspicious."

"And when was the last time that happened?" Troy asked.

"About a month ago," she admitted. "A man wrote to her and stated how he admired her for her work in cleansing the area. It was flagged, then sent to the authorities and my father. Nothing ever came of it."

"I'd like the details regarding that."

"You've got what I have in those files, but you also have access to everything at the county. But the gentleman in question has done nothing wrong besides spewing a few hateful words about sex workers. Questioning him at this point would be considered harassment until I can rule the fire arson."

"I don't mean to bring up something painful, but wasn't one of the things that sent your mom over the edge the fact your father was arrested for being with a prostitute?" Trent asked.

Esme nodded. "She felt betrayed by what he'd done and thought it was her calling to rid the world of those who sold their bodies. The only problem with that was somewhere in her skewed thinking, she believed I was somehow a demon seed."

Troy muttered a few superlatives under his breath. "I'm sorry."

"I'm not. That fire brought me together with the only father I've ever known. Weirdly, I'm grateful for that."

"I suppose I can understand that," Troy said.

"Well, I better be going. I'm meeting Sparrow at my dad's place to review some of his things. If I come across anything I think can be useful to the case, I'll call."

"We'll do the same." Troy waved the folders. "Thanks for these. I'll see you tomorrow at the interview."

He raced across the hood of her car and opened the door, ignoring the glares from his brothers. "Drive safe."

"See you tomorrow." Esme climbed up into the driver's seat and pressed the ignition button. The engine roared to life.

He waited until Esme was out of sight before facing the firing squad. "I'm going to head to the stables. I need to go over Billy's record from start to finish."

Trent stared at him with that all-knowing superpower twin look.

God. Troy hated that look.

Marcus shook his head. "Don't do it. The last thing you need is to crash and burn."

"Have a little faith in our brother's game," Heath said. "But yeah. I agree. The timing is off. You should wait."

"I'm not going to call her." He held up his finger. "Unless it's for work. So all you yahoos can get your heads out of your asses and go do whatever it is you do when the sun goes down. I've got work to do." He pivoted on his heel and stomped off toward the stable.

He hoped the files were riveting and full of exciting details.

Because his mind was still following that Jeep down the driveway.

CHAPTER 4

ESME JADE STARED into the fireplace and watched the flames dance like a disco ball. The temperature outside had only dropped to sixty-eight degrees. Most people wouldn't consider starting a fire in June. Not even in Colorado. But Esme's father loved to sit in front of one with a glass of scotch and a good book.

Lifting the glass in the air, she turned her attention to her friend. "Here's to my dad. One of the good guys."

"I'll drink to that," Sparrow said. She tossed back her head and downed half of hers as if it were a shot. She pounded the center of her chest.

"It's meant to be sipped. Not chugged." Esme laughed. Scotch wasn't her drink of choice. She preferred Tennessee whiskey. But tonight was all about honoring her father. Tears stung the corners of her eyes.

Henri Jade was gone.

She'd never see him again. She'd never have to listen to his stupid jokes or be reminded that she'd yet to give him a grandchild. Something that they both had wanted, though he was in more of a hurry for her to find her life partner and settle down than she had been.

But now she had no one to walk her down the aisle when it did happen. A thought that sent her heart to the center of her throat.

"You forget who my father is," Sparrow said. "He never *sipped* anything in his life. Basically, he opened his mouth and poured in the alcohol like a wide-open fire hydrant."

Some might have found the comment distasteful, considering how Esme's father died. However, Esme and Sparrow shared a common bond that most couldn't understand.

Esme's back tightened. She rubbed her right biceps. While her life differed from Sparrow's, they both grew up living in a world where people wondered if they might end up just like their mothers.

Criminals.

Sparrow also had a father who used to be a criminal and often people wondered if he still had ties to the Renegades. Still, Sparrow was a well-respected officer of the law and married to a man who worked for the Brotherhood Protectors. Sparrow had proven to the Fool's Gold community that she would always protect them.

No matter what.

Esme hadn't had to prove herself in the same way. She had no recollection of the first two years of her life. Her muscles twitched. They remembered her mother.

The beatings.

The leather belt across her back.

Sleeping in a cage meant for a dog instead of a crib.

And then there was the fire that left the scars on her back and arm. The same fire where her father had scooped her up into his arms and carried her out to safety. He rode with her in the ambulance and stayed in the hospital, where she was treated for second-degree burns, malnutrition, and dehydration.

Weeks later he took her home, adopted her, and raised her as his own.

He never lied to her about where she came from and even allowed her to visit her biological mother when Esme was fifteen and started asking questions. He stood by her side and supported her when she needed him the most. She couldn't remember a time in her life when he wasn't there.

Until now.

"Speaking of your dad," Esme said, avoiding the

topic of her mother's crazy admirer. "He and Anna Marie stopped by earlier with some flowers. They seem really happy together."

"They are and I'm so glad my dad found someone who can see past who he used to be, though she still struggles with how people treat him sometimes, but that often has to do with the fact he still refuses to remove or alter that damn tattoo."

"Yeah. People see the Renegade symbol and it terrifies them." Esme had to admit that Albert Oakley could be intimidating as all hell. Just looking at him could make a person want to turn and run the other way. However, once anyone spent five minutes with the man, they understood that he was sweet and kind and would do anything for those he loved. "But your dad has proven himself time and again in this community. I don't understand why some people don't trust him. Especially after what happened last year."

"I stopped trying to figure it out." Sparrow shrugged. "So, are you going to tell me why I'm here?"

"My mom has a new crazy and my dad was keeping it from me," Esme blurted out.

"I haven't heard anything, but unless they send someone from my office, they often keep me out of the loop because of our friendship."

It wasn't the first time her father had protected her from the insanity that was her mother. But it had been the first time he hadn't even told her after the fact. "I've never understood why my dad did stuff like that. I'm a big girl and can handle all the weird shit my mom and her crazies do."

"Do you think this one might be connected to the fire?" Sparrow leaned forward.

"I don't know and I have very few details. I mentioned it to Troy and his brothers. I wanted them to have the full picture, but so far, I can't find much on it. I will send you what I do have, and maybe you can find out more."

"What's the name?"

"Chuck Manzo," Esme said.

"Shit. I know that name. My office didn't handle it, but I remember Jim talking all hush-hush about it. I'll get the official file, but if your dad has unofficial shit, send it to me."

Esme wished she had more than a page of hand-written notes on a police report. "I haven't found much and I want to keep it quiet. The last thing I need is for this to be a media circus around my mom, so whatever you do, be discreet."

"Absolutely."

"The thing is, that fire was no accident, and if by chance Chuck Manzo, the man who has been writing to my mom, has anything to do with why my father was in that building, well, I've got to find that out." Esme took another slow sip, letting the scotch fill her mouth before she swallowed.

"I'll do what I can on my end."

"I have no proof that it was arson. Yet. But something doesn't feel right; however, it also doesn't feel like my mother."

"I'm not going to disagree with you, on both counts."

"It's going to be hard to prove arson. Even harder to figure out who started it."

"I'll keep it as a crime scene for as long as possible," Sparrow said. "Jim told me to put all my best people on it and to give you whatever you need."

"I appreciate that." She leaned forward, setting her glass on the coffee table, and lifted all the preliminary reports from the fire, which were paper-thin and inconclusive. Arson was by far one of the hardest things to prove, unless a firefighter could definitively say that a fire had been behaving uncharacteristically or an accelerant had been used. Or perhaps more than one point of origin could be located.

But otherwise, half the time, the fire destroyed all the evidence, making her job that much harder.

"If we find something, it's possible my boss could take me off the case," Esme said. George Armond frequently was more concerned about how things might look. If it turns out that the fire was set on purpose *and* there was reason to believe that her father was targeted, then George might pull her faster than a speeding bullet.

"I'll talk to George." Sparrow stood. "I'll make sure

that doesn't happen. Or if it does, I'll get Jim to sign off on having you as a consultant to the sheriff's department."

"Let's hope it doesn't come to that."

Sparrow nodded. "I hate to do this, but I need to get home. Call me if you need anything."

"Will do." Esme pushed herself to a standing position and followed Sparrow to the front door. They had known each other since they were little girls. When all the other children on the playground were told to stay far away from Sparrow, Esme's father encouraged her to be kind.

The two girls bonded over being misfits and having mothers who didn't protect them, but fathers who loved them dearly.

"I'm here for you. Don't you ever forget it." Sparrow pulled Esme in for a bear hug.

Esme wrapped her arms around her lifelong friend. She wasn't one for crocodile tears or embraces that went on forever. However, tonight she needed to feel loved.

She needed that connection to someone who cared and not just because she'd lost her father. "Thank you," she managed, holding the emotion close to her chest. As much as she wanted to cry, she wasn't going to. She'd save that for her pillow later.

"I'll check in with you after Billy's interview."

Esme pulled open the door and stood there until Sparrow not only got in her vehicle and backed out of the driveway, but she waited for the taillights to disappear in the distance.

She turned, locked the door, and returned to her dad's family room where she picked up a stack of papers from the coffee table. She lifted her glass and poured herself another drink. The fire crackled in the background. Growing up, she used to love to sit on the floor and play with her log set and fire trucks, pretending to put out a blaze while her dad read one of his favorite novels.

Tucking the papers under her arm, she strolled down the hallway toward her father's office. A million memories danced in her mind.

Her father standing at the back doorway by the garage as she came down the back staircase in her prom dress.

Or the time he blindfolded her so he could surprise her with a new SUV on her eighteenth birthday.

A single tear streaked down her cheek as she rounded the corner and stepped into her dad's sanctuary. She let it hang on the side of her face until it dripped to the floor with a tiny splash. Pictures of her and all her accomplishments filled the room.

Every father loved their baby girl.

Esme didn't feel as though Henri Jade loved her more than any other dad. But he did have a way of making her feel as though she was special. That he somehow handpicked her to be *his* daughter. Their bond was so strong that they could sense when the other was hurting, both emotionally and physically.

It's like a twin connection.

Or at least that's what she'd called it.

Her dad had called it intuition.

Running her finger over the thick wood desk, she could still smell her father's dense musky aftershave. It filled her nostrils and she sneezed.

"Speak to me, Daddy." She maneuvered to the other side and sat in the big black leather chair. Sipping her scotch, she studied the reports and notes taken from the fire.

Two off-duty firefighters from the Fool's Gold Fire Station had been the first on the scene.

She lifted a pen and circled a question that still needed to be answered.

What was Henri Jade doing at a condemned building at seven in the evening?

This particular building was scheduled for demolition in a week. Everything was good to go. There was no reason for her father to be inside it.

She pulled out the hand-drawn map of Fool's Gold. The building was located a half mile outside of town and not far from the Bottom of the Barrel Tavern. Her father had been known to go there a time or two for a drink and it was a known watering hole for many firefighters since it wasn't too far from the fire station. If something had happened to her dad as he *walked* by the building, well, that might be a different story.

But he had been inside.

The first question that had to be answered.

She circled another question that tickled her brain.

What did Micky Glass see while inside the building?

Currently, Micky was heavily sedated and on a ventilator after undergoing surgery to have five ribs plated after falling through the floorboards of the second story. He also had a broken leg and a broken wrist. First responders had pulled him out.

And then there was Billy.

He hadn't given an official statement. She flipped the page of her notebook and wrote what she knew about what had happened.

Billy and Micky arrived at the scene at six thirty and noticed the fire chief's car parked in front of the condemned building, which was on fire.

They called the fire department immediately.

They entered through the unlocked front door.

It was filled with smoke and all rooms were already lit up.

Billy climbed through the window at six fifty-one where first responders met him.

Micky was pulled from the burning building at six fifty-three.

The fire was put out by eight twenty when the chief's body was found.

Billy swore he never saw Henri Jade.

Her dad's body was found in the living room. The fire was believed to have been started in the kitchen.

The building was ancient and a pile of kindling. She wasn't surprised it went up in flames quickly.

But she was surprised at how quickly the fire was contained. Not that she questioned the competency of the Fools Gold Fire Department. She knew they were top-notch. But a fire of that caliber should take hours to control and put out.

That indicted accelerant could have been used, not giving the fire a chance to take hold of the wood, forcing the fire to flame out as it was doused with water.

A noise—like a door opening and closing—caught her attention. She stood, found her weapon, and slinked out from behind the desk. She peered into the hallway, checking both directions. One led to the far staircase and the other back to the living room. It had been a few years since she'd been a cop, but she used all her skills to home in on every noise in the house.

She could hear the crackle of the fire in the other room.

A slight breeze rustled the trees outside.

Her nerves were shot.

She turned, sighed, and headed back toward her father's desk when something hard came down on the back of her head.

She groaned as she dropped to her knees. She blinked. The weapon in her hands fell to the floor. The room spun before everything faded to black.

TROY'S HEART raced as he leaped from the front of his pickup and jogged across the walkway.

"You must be the new fire chief," a man standing at the front door said.

"And you are?"

"Stone Bishop. A fellow Brotherhood Protectors agent."

"It's a pleasure meeting you." Troy stretched out his hand. "What the hell happened? Where's Esme? Is she okay? When she called, she mentioned she'd been knocked out."

"She's with Sparrow in her father's office. I was instructed to wait for you."

Troy followed Stone inside the modest home that had belonged to his predecessor. Even if Troy was only the acting chief for a short period, it was a role he took seriously. When he'd left the Air Force to take care of his father, he had every intention of seeking employment in the field in a management role.

He never expected to be thrust into this type of position so quickly, and he figured once they understood what happened to Henri, he'd be dumped back to the station to work under his brother, Seth.

Wonderful.

However, until that happened, he had a job and planned on going above and beyond the call of duty.

It had nothing to do with the fact that he was insanely attracted to Esme in ways he hadn't been to a woman in years. It wasn't her good looks either that had gotten under his skin. It was how she carried herself and the respect she commanded from those who knew her well.

However, there were a couple who didn't like her or who appeared jealous.

That was to be expected.

"This might be a silly question, but why aren't there any official police cars?" Troy asked.

"Sparrow—and Esme—decided that handling this quietly might be better, just in case this has something to do with Henri's death."

"What do you think?"

"I've learned not to argue with my wife about her job and she doesn't pick fights with me about mine."

"And when they overlap, like this one?"

Stone chuckled. "For now, keeping things on the down-low is for the best. We have no idea what we're dealing with. Or what the intruder was looking for or if they even found it. You do have the authority to override me. You're the lead Brotherhood agent on this case. If you want to call in for backup, we can."

"I don't know enough about what's going on to make that call and that's troublesome for so many reasons," Troy admitted. "Keeping things hush-hush for the time being works for me, but I need to get a good look at everything. Hell, I've barely been in Henri's office I've been so busy with other things."

"I've got your back," Stone said. "So does Sparrow. Anything you need, just let us know."

"Thanks," Troy said. "Does Esme know how long the interloper was here?"

"About twenty minutes," Stone said. "She glanced at her watch before she got up to check on a noise. She was unconscious for approximately eighteen minutes."

"A doctor should see her."

"I'm fine," Esme's voice rang out loud and clear. She stepped into the family room wearing jeans and a white T-shirt. Her long blond hair flowed softly over her shoulders.

"You have a concussion. The question is, how bad?" Troy swallowed as he stared into her beautiful blue eyes. He leaned against the wall near the front door.

"That's what I told her, but she's about as stubborn as I am." Sparrow entered the room and joined her husband, wrapping her arm around his waist. "We couldn't find anything missing, but we don't know what he had in his office either. Whoever was here went through all the files, dumped them out, and left."

"What about the rest of the house?" Troy inched closer to Esme, trying to get a look at the back of her head. A trickle of blood clung to her hair.

"I did a walk-through and it doesn't appear they went anywhere other than his office," Stone said.

"Whatever they wanted, they thought it would be there." Esme glanced up at him and crinkled her nose. "The question is, what?"

"And is it related to that house fire," Troy added. "You need ice on that." He peered over the top of her head, examining it to ensure she didn't need stitches, but the wound wasn't that bad. However, she did have a nice-sized bump.

"I'm fine. Really. You can stop being an old maid." Esme narrowed her stare.

He ignored the jab. "What about a police presence during the night?"

"I've already called the deputy on tonight and they will be driving by often, but I don't have the manpower to put someone on the house twenty-four seven," Sparrow said.

"That should be fine." Esme winced when she touched the back of her head.

"I'll spend the night." Troy almost regretted the words the second they left his tongue.

"The hell you will." Esme glared.

"Sweetheart, I think this is our cue to leave." Stone

took Sparrow's hand and guided her to the front door. "Call us if you need anything. Day or night."

"Take your buddy with you," Esme said.

"Nope. He belongs to you right now." Stone laughed. "And that's an order."

Troy did the honor of walking Stone and Sparrow to the door, locking it after they left. He turned and took one step before pausing.

"You're not staying here tonight." Esme folded her arms and cocked her head. "I don't need a babysitter."

"I'm your bodyguard and while my team was first brought in for this case, I wasn't supposed to be with you twenty-four seven, and it still won't be possible with me as acting fire chief, but this changes things."

"I don't need you staying over."

"Jake Cogburn feels differently." He pulled out his cell and handed it to her with the text message he'd received when he'd arrived. "I'm under direct orders to stay put for the evening. Now, you don't want to get me in trouble with my new boss, do you?"

She stared at the phone for a long moment and sighed. "Fine. But only because everyone at your organization has always been a friend to my dad— and to me—and I could use a hand cleaning up the mess in my dad's office, but not tonight. I'm too tired."

"I wouldn't mind going through his office, if you don't mind."

"Knock yourself out."

He followed her down the hallway, which was lined with pictures of her when she'd been younger. Images of her playing soccer. A few of her during her days as a young firefighter. A police officer.

It appeared she was the pride and joy of her dad.

His heart squeezed.

His old man didn't have pictures of his kids. Hell, he could barely tell them apart, especially him and Trent, which was hysterical given the fact they weren't identical.

Esme grieved a great man who loved her dearly.

Troy grieved the idea of a father who didn't care enough to even come to his wedding—that never happened. He paused at the end of the hallway and ran his fingers over the last picture of Esme and her dad.

"That was taken three months ago," Esme whispered. She stood so close he could feel her breath tickle his skin. "We'd gone out to dinner to celebrate my birthday. I was hoping to talk him into letting me fix him up on a date. He lost his wife a while back and he seemed so lonely, but he said he wasn't ready yet."

"You had a special relationship with your dad."

"He was my world," she said. "Three weeks ago, I noticed he started pulling away from me, but I didn't have a good handle on it and now I'm wondering if maybe it could be related to his death."

"What do you mean?" Troy turned, resting his

hands on her shoulders, rolling his thumbs gingerly, doing his best to soak in whatever pain of hers that he could.

"It started when he wouldn't call me back right away. Or answer my texts as quickly. We both got busy with work and after his wife died, he often got withdrawn, so I gave him space. However, as I go back and examine his last weeks, something was off. I should have known." Tears filled her sweet, sensitive eyes.

Troy considered himself a good judge of character and while he believed every word that came from Esme's mouth, he also knew that she was withholding something important.

"Oh no. Don't do this to yourself." He ran his hands up and down her arms. "Hindsight, while in some cases can be a good thing, other times it's dangerous and only fucks with our minds."

"You sound like Sparrow."

"She's a smart woman," Troy said, wiping away a tear that dribbled down her cheek. "I'm going to help you figure all this out, but you have to promise me you're not going to keep second-guessing your actions leading up to your father's death. You did nothing wrong and while I didn't know your dad, I bet he was the kind of man who would hate you blaming yourself."

"You're right about that." She inhaled sharply.

He leaned in and gently brushed his lips across

hers in a warm kiss. He didn't let them linger too long. He didn't want to give her the wrong impression, even though that's exactly what he wanted. He had to keep things professional, but he also wanted to be compassionate.

"Thank you for understanding." She took a step back.

"One thing I'd like for you to do by morning is to get me a list of people who might have a vendetta against your dad."

"I already started working on it."

"Good," he said.

"I'm going to turn in. Your room is up the stairs, second door on the left," she said. "I'm right across the hall."

"Good night, Esme." He watched as she made her way toward the staircase. She turned and smiled before disappearing.

Damn.

He had to get his head on straight. He headed for her father's office. He needed a distraction from his inappropriate thoughts. Hopefully, he'd be able to find some direction in a case that had not one single lead. Worse, technically, her father's death wasn't currently considered anything other than a tragic accident.

Something his gut knew wasn't true.

Now all he had to do was find the facts to back it up.

CHAPTER 5

TROY SAT at the kitchen table. It felt strange to have spent the night at Henri Jade's house. He hadn't slept more than thirty minutes at a time. Between his mind's inability to shut off regarding the fire and all the pieces that didn't fit together, and his body's wicked reaction and uncontrolled lust for Esme, he had to find a way to get her out of this house.

He understood that bringing her anywhere wouldn't change his attraction, but he wouldn't be reminded of her at every turn. Hell, the soap in the shower smelled of her.

So did the towel that he dried himself off with.

When he stepped from the bathroom, his eyes were assaulted with pictures.

He couldn't go anywhere in this home without seeing or feeling her presence.

At least back at his stable, it would his home. His smells. And he'd have his brothers to keep him in check.

Now all he had to do was find a way to talk her into it.

The problem was that he didn't know her that well. He didn't know her blind spot. He had no idea what key points to use to make her see that staying here was a bad idea.

He couldn't use the bad guys would be back because they probably wouldn't. If they didn't find what they were looking for the first time with her in the house, they'd look elsewhere.

The question was, where was that?

Perhaps his office.

But that wasn't going to be so easy to get into.

The sounds of squeaky stair boards pulled him from his thoughts. He reached for the coffee mug and took a long slow sip. He stared at all the papers he'd taken from her father's office, along with the notes he'd started.

There were too many unanswered questions. The first one was, did she know her father was contemplating letting Billy go? The paperwork wasn't in Billy's file. But Troy had found a handwritten sticky note on a folder in the chief's office. The note read: *Should I actually fire Billy this time or not? Yes or no?* Considering the history and how close she was with her dad, he wondered if he would have confided in her. Or was this why he was distant? And what made this time different than all the other times Billy had been suspended or reprimanded?

Troy's hackles stood at attention. He wondered more about Billy and it solidified his decision not to reinstate him anytime soon.

"Did you sleep okay?" Esme asked as she entered the room. She smelled of peaches and cream. Her damp blond hair flowed over her shoulders. She wore a touch of makeup around her eyes and her lips were a pale pink. Her dark slacks hugged her hips, showing off her womanly figure. Her white sleeveless V-neck shirt clung to her body, leaving him remembering all the inappropriate dreams that danced in his mind like a broken record.

Damn, he had it bad.

"I wish I could lie and say I did. But I have a horrible habit of being way too honest."

She pulled down a mug and put it under the machine, pushing a few buttons. Leaning against the counter, she folded her arms while she waited for her coffee to brew. "I can't say I got much either."

"Are you worried whoever attacked you will come back?"

"Yes and no."

The coffee machine gurgled as it dripped out the last few drops. She snagged the cup and made her way to the table, picking the chair directly across from him.

"More yes or more no?" he asked, trying to get a read on her professionally. Her blue eyes were filled with thick, raw emotion. That was to be expected. She'd lost her father. A man who she revered. Admired. Respected. Someone who had protected her for most of her life.

Henri had been the kind of father Troy had hoped he'd be until Darlene destroyed his hopes and dreams.

"Do you remember when I told you about the man writing to my mother?"

Troy nodded.

She pulled out her cell and tapped the screen. "I haven't spoken to my mother in ten years and while I've always asked for any correspondence that is questionable to be sent my way, I tend to ignore it unless it's red-flagged."

"You mentioned yesterday that one was, but after an investigation, it wasn't taken seriously." Troy took her phone and glanced at a document.

Chuck Manzo.

Writes to Heather Roman regularly.

Admired her work in cleansing the world of evil, especially prostitutes.

He describes his mother as a whore who welcomes evil in her bed.

Troy continued to scroll, paying close attention to the handwritten notes in the margins.

Why does he describe how each place Heather burned looks like now? What is the significance of that?

Why doesn't she acknowledge that in her letters back?

"What am I looking at?" Troy glanced up over the electronic device.

"My father's notes on the crazy man who is still writing to my mom," Esme said. "I confirmed that yesterday with the warden of the prison."

"I thought you were informed of all letters that were suspicious. Is this man still writing to your mother?"

"He is and it turns out, my father asked the powers that be to keep me in the dark, especially since the sheriff's office did a thorough investigation and while the guy has some issues, he appears harmless."

"I don't like the word *appear*," Troy said. "My father *appeared* to be one of the good guys and when it came to fighting fires, he was. But he was a shit dad." Troy grimaced. That was completely inappropriate. He should have bit his tongue, or at the very least, made a different analogy. "What did Jim and his team find out about this Chuck Manzo fella?"

"For starters, Heather isn't the only one he writes to who's incarcerated."

Troy arched a brow. "Another arsonist?"

She took a sip of her coffee before answering. "No. A man who murdered seven people who he believed were possessed by the devil."

"I see." Troy pinched the bridge of his nose. "I take it Chuck praised this man for his work in cleansing the area."

"Exactly. However, the tone of the letters is different. It seems Chuck has romantic feelings for my mom. He feels they are connected and in his letters he states it's obvious she should know why. My mom always responds back with some scripture reading, but never states she gets the connection."

"When was the last time your dad visited your mom?"

"Ew." Esme scrunched up her face as if she bit into an unexpected sour flavor. "We never refer to Heather as mom when referencing my dad. It makes it sound as if they both produced me."

"Okay." Troy understood that Heather and a man by the name of Kirk Roman had been her biological parents, but she constantly spoke about Heather as her mom, so he didn't quite get it, but he'd roll with it.

"The warden told me my dad saw her three days before he died."

"I think I need to pay a visit to Heather," Troy said.

"She won't see you."

"Why not?"

"Because you have nothing to offer her." Esme raised her finger. "However, she'll see me and you can come with. It might piss her off, and she'll play games, but we might get something out of her that way."

"Speaking of things to do together." Troy downed the last gulp of his coffee, wishing he had shot of whiskey in it. "Don't forget I want to be present today for your interview with Billy."

She tilted her head. "I've been thinking about that, and I'm not sure it's necessary. As a matter of fact, I'd prefer you weren't there. I think that might make him defensive."

He reached across the table and tapped Billy's file, one of the things he'd spent his morning reading. It seemed odd to Troy that the exit papers for the department weren't in Billy's file. "Half of his insubordination complaints have to do with following orders—from women." Troy lowered his chin. "I want to see how he responds to you and your questions." There was more to it than that, but he'd start there.

"There's something about my past with Billy you should know."

"Oh? What's that?" Troy swallowed. He didn't like where his mind went. Or worse, his gut, which in this case, he trusted as much as he trusted facts.

"He was my high school sweetheart."

"No offense, but I struggle to see the attraction." Troy was afraid of that.

"You and everyone else in this town," she admitted. "My father never liked him, but not because of me. Once Billy and I started working together, things got difficult. He struggled with the way people treated me."

Troy gripped his mug. "Please don't tell me the men in your station house were assholes."

She laughed. "No. The complete opposite. But it was the way I excelled at everything and Billy was always one step behind me. I'm not trying to be arrogant, believe me. I'm not a highly competitive person, but Billy is and he needs all the accolades. He needs to be a hero. He needs to have that special pat on the back and my father never gave it to him. Instead, my dad suspended him at every turn. He didn't fire him because at the end of the day, Billy is a good firefighter."

"I read that three times Billy has gone for captain and been denied."

Esme nodded. "I'm sure he's pissed that your brother Seth came in and took it."

"Seth's been a captain. He has the experience and he's never been suspended for any reason." Troy stiffened his spine. He didn't have to defend his brother so adamantly. Seth's record spoke volumes about the type of man Seth had become. "Besides, I couldn't name someone who was suspended."

81

She held up both hands. "I wouldn't expect you to name Billy, ever. He's arrogant and not a leader. And that wasn't my point. All I'm saying is that because he doesn't always respond well to authority, and you're his new boss, who by the looks of it, you can't be more than a year or two older than he is—"

"And how old is that?"

"He and I are both thirty-three."

"I'm a year older," Troy said.

"Billy has always resented my career and he'll resent the hell out of you as fire chief at thirty-four. He will hold his temper for as long as he can. He will answer my questions professionally, until he can't. And if you have no intention of putting him back in the rotation, he might have a few choice words for both of us."

"I'll be honest, I have no intention of reinstating him this week. I might not do it until after we know how the fire was started." He wasn't sure he was going to fire him either. Troy needed more information.

She jerked her head. "You don't think he had anything to do with it?"

"I have no reason to believe he did. But Micky will be unconscious for at least another three days. Maybe longer. I want to hear his account of what happened before I make any decisions, but I'm not telling Billy that," Troy said. "Unfortunately, the doctors are telling me it could be a while before he's stable enough to handle questions."

"Is there something you're not telling me? Because if there is, that would be irresponsible of you. This is not only my father's death we're talking about, but also my investigation."

Troy reached across the table and took her hand. "When it comes to the fire investigation, I will take my lead from you. However, I'm in charge of the fire department and while your dad had his reasons for keeping someone like Billy on, his record doesn't sit well with me."

"Can I ask you a question?"

"Of course."

"If you had walked by that building that night and saw one of your brothers' vehicles parked outside, are you telling me you would have stood outside and waited for backup?"

Troy released her hand and stood.

Go. Take your brothers. I'll be right behind you. I promise.

His mother's words forever burned into his memory.

Reluctantly, Seth had grabbed him by one hand and Trent by the other, dragging them out of their home.

Troy had glanced over his shoulder once, watching his mother disappear into the flames. That was the last memory he had of his mother alive.

"My initial first reaction to that question is no." He rinsed out his mug and turned. Talking about what happened to his mom didn't often bring such raw emotion to the surface. Perhaps it had to do with what had happened to her father and the way in which he'd died. Or how much love filled the room when she spoke of her dad. "I say that only because my mother died in a house fire after trying to save our grandfather."

"I'm so sorry."

"I was just a kid," he said. "My mother sent me, my twin, and Seth out the door while she went back to get Grandpa. Neither one made it and that's why I say I wouldn't do it without proper backup. But I'm not a fool. My brothers mean everything to me and I know I'd lay down my life for them."

"At least you're honest."

"Here's another dose of honesty for you," he said. "I don't believe, at least from what you've told me and what I've read, that Billy does anything unless it benefits him. That means, he doesn't run into a burning building unless he's getting something from it."

"What are you saying?"

"If he didn't believe your dad was in there, he would have called for backup." While Troy never acted on his gut instincts without facts when it came to an investigation, he did trust them when it came to people.

His gut told him that Esme was as solid as they came.

And Billy was an arrogant man looking for a payday. That didn't necessarily come in the form of money, but he wasn't the kind of man who did something out of the goodness of his heart.

"He's been suspended before for doing shit like that."

Troy nodded. "Yeah. But important people were behind the doors. Or he had an audience." Quickly, he moved across the room and flipped open the file. "I found two emergency situations where he didn't go racing in and called 9-1-1. He followed protocol."

"He does that sometimes. Usually right after he's been reinstated."

"That may be the case, but what I found interesting was that in both these incidents, there was no possibility of injury or loss of life. I don't want a man on a team with my brothers who suffers from hero syndrome."

"If he truly had that, then he's been creating these situations, and while Billy is a bit of a dick, he wouldn't do anything that put someone in harm's way, except maybe himself."

"I'm going to state it empathically, and for the record. As his boss, I want to be there when you interview him." Troy blew out a breath. "I'm happy to let you use my office."

She leaned back in her chair, holding his gaze

with a contemplative glare. "All right. But I need you to let me conduct it without interference. You can't interrupt me."

"What if I have questions?"

"We'll have to come up with a system, because you have tapped into one valid point about Billy's personality. If we don't look as though we're united on all fronts, he'll use it against us."

Troy hadn't thought about how his presence might make her look in front of Billy and the last thing he wanted was for her position to be compromised in any way. "Why don't we take the time to make a list of questions that we want answered. Compare them, see if they jog any more, and we can go from there. However, you have my word that this is your investigation. I won't do anything that will make him think otherwise. I will make it clear that my role is to learn about the department and how things work, since I'm new."

"Thank you."

"Now, I have one more thing I need to discuss with you and I don't think you're going to like it." Troy chose to continue to stand. It was a power thing, but sometimes he did his best debating on his feet.

"I can already tell, I'm going to hate it, whatever it is."

He chuckled. He couldn't remember a time he felt this comfortable with a lady. Esme had that certain something that made him at ease. She spoke with confidence and intelligence that spoke to his soul. "I'd like to take all your father's files to Paradise Ranch."

"That's not an outrageous demand."

"I'd like you to come too," he said. "We have no clue if whoever broke in will be back, but they have no reason to come to me."

"You want me to come stay with you and your brothers?" Her brows shot up.

"I can keep you safe there."

She glanced around the kitchen and shrugged. "Okay."

His lips parted and he blinked. "I expected to have to toss you over my shoulder and drag you out of here kicking and screaming."

The corners of her mouth curved into a wicked smile. "I'd like to see you try."

"Are you propositioning me?" His heart lurched to the back of his throat before dropping to his heels. "Because it wouldn't take much."

"This conversation went south real quick." She pushed her chair back. "I need to go pack a few things. I'll be ready to go in a half hour." She waltzed past him, but paused at the opening of the hallway and turned. "Do you all live in that big house together and where am I sleeping?"

"Seth has the house. I live in the stables. You'll obviously be staying with me and don't worry, you can have my bed. I'll take the blowup mattress in the office."

"Stables? This I have to see." She disappeared down the hallway.

What the hell had he gotten himself into?

CHAPTER 6

Esme sat behind what used to be her father's desk, but now belonged to Troy Falco. Fool's Gold Fire Department had already removed her dad's name from the door and put Troy's name on it.

She doubted he would remain as the acting fire chief.

Not if they were already putting his stamp on things around the office.

She didn't begrudge him the title. Not at all. The department needed a good man to fill her father's shoes and Troy had the backing of the Brotherhood Protectors. That said something.

"Are you listening to me?" Sparrow barked in her ear.

"Yes. I heard you. I'll send you my notes as soon as I'm done."

"That's not what I asked."

"Oh. What then?"

"You're staying at Paradise Ranch? With Troy? Did something happen last night?"

Esme exhaled sharply. "No. And how do you know I'm staying there? That's supposed to be top secret."

"Don't worry. It's still classified, but Stone is running the office for Jake for the next couple of weeks and you know our jobs often collide. This is one of those times. But I want to know how he talked you into staying there."

"The truth is I don't want to be alone." Of all the people in the world, Esme knew she could tell Sparrow anything. Over the years, they had cried on each other's shoulders. They had been there for the other when no one else would have dared show up. "Being at my father's house was proving too hard, and going back and forth to Colorado Springs would be too daunting, especially when George told me I could run the investigation from here as long as I kept Colby in the loop."

"You chose a sexy stranger over me? I'm hurt." Sparrow's tone had a sense of humor laced to it.

"He's not a stranger."

"At least you're agreeing he's sexy."

"I'm going to tell your husband you think the new fire chief is hot." A noise caught her attention, and she shifted the chair toward the door.

She gasped.

There stood Troy with a smile. He winked.

"I gotta go." Esme swallowed the thick lump that had formed in her throat. "I'll send over that report when I'm done. Let's touch base later so we can compare notes."

"So, Sparrow thinks I'm something to look at. Do you agree?"

"I'm not answering that."

"It would probably be considered inappropriate," he teased.

"Not probably. Definitely."

"I'm sorry. I didn't mean anything by it," he said.

"Oh, my God. No. I'm the one who should be apologizing. I know you were simply following my conversation with Sparrow. I didn't mean to make you feel bad."

"Before Billy arrives, let's get this out in the open." He jumped to his feet, closed the door, and leaned against the wood barrier.

Her heart hammered in her chest. She couldn't tell where one beat started and another one stopped. She had no idea what he wanted to bring to the surface, but she suspected it had to do with how she wanted to throw caution to the wind and kiss him until their clothes magically fell to the floor.

"I've never been in an employment situation where I found my co-worker not only attractive, but someone I wanted to spend time with outside of work."

"Did you come to this conclusion before or after you invited me to your stable?"

"That's a fair question." He chuckled. "My thought process on that is twofold. I know the ranch better than your father's house. I feel that I can keep you safe there. Plus, it doesn't smell like you."

"Excuse me?" She cocked her head.

"Everywhere I turned at your dad's place reminded me of you somehow. I thought it would be easier for me at Paradise Ranch. But seeing you sitting behind a desk that I spent all morning making mine has made me realize that it will be impossible to avoid the fact that I find you irresistible."

"I've never met anyone as honest as you and I'm starting to wonder if there's a hidden agenda behind it."

"Nope. I'd rather you know that I'm feeling these things." He held up his hands. "Which I have no intention of acting upon, then try to hide them and somehow either insult you or worse. We have to work together. You have an investigation to lead, and I need to protect and support you. That's the most important thing through all this."

Esme had never been put in this kind of position before. She wasn't sure how to respond. Being honest with a man about her emotions wasn't something she'd done in years.

If ever.

She protected her heart, and with good reason.

The moment anyone found out who she was, they guarded themselves. There had only been one man that point-blank asked her if she ever had thoughts about lighting him on fire in the middle of the night.

She broke up with him on the spot.

Others tried to pretend it didn't bother them, and even if it didn't, her heritage always got in the way of someone in their family, ending the relationship because they couldn't be involved with someone who had a hardened criminal for a mother.

"This isn't the best place to have this conversation," she started, "but I do find myself thinking about you in ways I shouldn't."

He smiled like a big goofy kid.

"I don't want to burst your bubble, but I'm also grieving and I find myself looking for ways to avoid feeling the pain."

"I understand what you're saying."

"Do you?"

He pushed from the door.

Shit. Gripping the armrests, she froze.

He held her gaze as he made his way across the room. He had this kindness about him that she wished she could ignore. The only other person she knew to be as genuine as him had been Sparrow.

But she certainly wasn't attracted to her best friend. At least not in a sexual way.

He twisted her chair and knelt in front of her, taking her hands in his big strong ones. "I barely remember my mom, but I miss her so much my heart hurts. Not a day goes by that I don't think about her, and it was brought to the surface when my father died. While I'm not avoiding my emotions over my dad's death, I grieved him my entire life. I'm diving into my job because I'll lose my mind if I don't. So, I do get that you're doing whatever it takes to get through the day. And the night."

She palmed his cheek. She could see right through his almond eyes and deep into his soul. If she were being totally honest, she could feel his genuine emotions fill her heart. She wanted to deny the connection—the bond—that developed seemingly overnight between them, but what would be the point? "I do find myself feeling things for you, but I don't know where to file them and—"

"Don't put them anywhere." He ran his thumb across her skin tenderly. "Knowledge is power. Having them out in the open allows us to work around them."

"Says the man who has his lips so close to mine I can taste his desire," she whispered.

His tongue peeked out from his mouth. She leaned closer. Her breath caught in the center of her chest. She wanted to kiss him so badly it burned her lungs.

Not the time or the place.

It was her father's voice that pulled her into reality.

But it was Troy who took a step back.

He stood, raking a hand through his hair. "For the record, I can feel your passion." He strolled to the door and gripped the handle. "I'm going to see if Billy is here yet. Can I get you anything?"

"A cold shower would be nice."

"I've got one of those at the stable."

"Do you want to know what the hardest part about all this is?" she asked.

He glanced over his shoulder. "Besides the obvious?"

She didn't dare respond to that comment, so she ignored it. "My father would have liked you."

He narrowed his stare. "I don't understand."

She opened her mouth to tell him about how her dad had never liked any man she dated and that he decided the first one he truly liked would be *the one*.

Troy Falco couldn't be that man.

It made no sense at all.

Except he was perfect.

A knock at the door made her snap her mouth shut.

"Chief Falco," his assistant, Ashley, said. "Billy Rocha is here to see Esme."

"You can tell him to come on back." Troy pulled one of the chairs to the right corner of the office. He sat down and crossed his legs.

They had gone over their game plan a half dozen times. This was not rocket science.

She opened her notebook and quickly glanced at all the information she'd gathered from the scene.

According to the firefighters at the scene, the fire had behaved irrationally.

Meaning it spread quickly.

It burned hot—as if there could be accelerant present, though that couldn't be proven so far and not everyone agreed. The building was old and a fire hazard to begin with.

"Esme," Billy said. "How are you holding up?"

"I'm doing okay." She stood, pressing her hands on the desk. "Thanks for coming. I know you want to get this over with."

"I hate doing it twice and then tracking down the new chief." He glanced in the direction of Troy. "Ashley didn't tell me you were here. Can we talk about my suspension when I'm done with this?"

Esme cringed. She knew Billy would put Troy on the spot and starting the interview off on this foot wasn't a good idea.

"I'm sorry, Billy. I wish I could have had that discussion today, but I haven't had a chance to review your file. Not to mention I have meetings all day and into tomorrow. We'll have to stick with our original plan and meet next week."

Billy slammed the door shut. "Do you have any idea how strapped you're leaving the station?"

"I have four brothers working there. If there's a real problem, Seth will let me know," Troy said.

"Your brothers are new. They don't know the way we do things here. You're making a big mistake." Billy plopped himself in the chair. "Esme, can we get started, please?"

"Sure." She scooted her chair a little closer. "Can you tell me what direction you were headed?"

"North," Billy said. "Micky and I parked in the free lot. As we were walking up the street, we noticed flames and as we were getting ready to call it in, we noticed your dad's vehicle."

Esme jotted down the first inconsistency in Billy's story.

It wasn't a big one, but it was still something to note because when she talked to him before, he said he noticed her father's car before he saw the flames.

"What did you do next?"

"Once we called it in, we went through the front door. The fire had consumed every room. It was running hot and black smoke was everywhere. We called for Henri. I went from the hallway into what I think was the dining room. I quickly realized that we weren't getting far and had to get out. When I turned to look for Micky, he was gone. I yelled for him. Nothing. I tried to get back to the front of the house, but couldn't." Billy ran his hand over his mouth. He did that when he got emotional. "I could feel the heat prickle my skin. I knew if I didn't get out, I'd be toast. I thought maybe Micky had the same feeling and had already left the building, so I found my escape out the back where my fellow firefighters greeted me, but no Micky." Billy lowered his head and sighed.

He wasn't good at faking his feelings. Actually, he sucked at it, so she knew these were real.

"If I had known he was still in there, I wouldn't have left."

"I know," Esme said softly. "What can you tell me about how the fire behaved?"

"It wasn't arson," Billy said. "That building was dry. It was like newspaper had been placed underneath the structure. It was ripe; all it needed was a flame to go up like kindling. I didn't see anything that would have made me think that it was anything other than a regular fire we see, unfortunately, every day."

"What about smells? No accelerant? Nothing out of the ordinary?" Esme asked.

"The only thing that struck me as odd was that your father was in the building," Billy said.

Her heart dropped to her toes. Tears stung the backs of her eyes, but she wouldn't let them break free.

"If you think of anything to add, please bring it to my attention."

"You know I will," Billy said. "Is there anything else? May I go?"

"You're free to leave," she said.

Billy stood. He turned and faced Troy. "Are you sure you don't have a few minutes?"

"Even if I did, it would not change the outcome. I

need time to go over your case." Troy pushed himself to a standing position. "We'll talk next week. Thanks for coming in."

Billy inched closer to Troy and puffed out his chest.

Esme inwardly groaned.

"You're putting good men at risk because you're on some power trip as the acting fire chief." Billy raised his hands, making air quotes. "Your title is temporary until Esme rules on the fire and we name an actual chief and it won't be you since you're incapable of doing your job properly." Billy turned and stormed out of the office.

"Well, we know how he feels about me." Troy leaned his ass against the desk. "What do you think about his statement?"

"He had some inconsistencies from when we talked to him at the scene, but they weren't anything I'd flag. However, his hostility was a little more aggressive than I would have expected considering the discussion we had."

"I'm not surprised," Troy said. "I wasn't honest with you about something in his file."

"What's that?"

"Your father was going to fire him. The question is, did he know?"

CHAPTER 7

TROY mentally prepared himself for two things. The first was explaining to Esme why he lied to her about the sticky note he found regarding Billy's possible dismissal from the Fool's Gold Fire Department. He had his reasons and was ready to defend them, although he wasn't about to bring up the topic of conversation. She would have to do that.

The second was all the shit he would take from his brothers for bringing Esme to the stables. He had all his one-liner comebacks ready to roll off his tongue about how he needed to protect her and it would be easier to do when he wasn't constantly looking over his shoulder, worried someone was going to break in. He and Stone had spent two hours setting up traps around Henri's home in case whoever attacked Esme decided to return. If they stayed there, he'd never sleep.

He chuckled as he glanced in the review mirror. He wasn't going to get much shut-eye anyway. He took the turn onto the gravel driveway. He and his brothers had talked about getting a big sign welcoming everyone to Paradise Ranch, but he'd settle for pavement.

Instead of pulling in front of the main house, he turned toward the stable and pulled around, parking on the backside. It didn't hide his vehicle, but it did camouflage it a bit.

He slid from behind the steering wheel and waved to Esme before snagging a pizza from the back seat along with a six-pack of beer.

She parked her Jeep and climbed out from the driver's side. "I can't wait to dig into that pie. I'm so hungry I can't hear myself think."

"Follow me." He strolled to the side door. All his life, he'd made sure he had at least two exits. It had never been about being afraid of a fire, or even feeling trapped. But being a firefighter and then an Air Force Fire Protection Specialist, he felt he had to practice what he preached.

Safety first.

And the first thing he'd done was ensure his home had been equipped to battle a fire.

There were not only fire extinguishers, but water access points.

However, the most important thing was that he and his brothers had a plan to ensure the maximum possibility of survival if something happened. That always cracked up Trent. He wasn't snubbing his nose at Troy's obsessive nature. No. He understood it. More so than any of his other brothers. But Trent hadn't come out of their shared trauma the same way, and considering they were twins, it was comical.

He tapped the combination on the keypad to unlock his door. It beeped and the lock clicked. Opening the door, he let Esme enter first while he desperately tried not to drop the pizza, which burned the palm of his hand it was so freaking hot.

"I can't believe you live here and not in the main house." She stood in the center and did a three-sixty. "This is an actual stable. Where you keep horses."

He laughed, making his way behind the office to the makeshift kitchen that had already been set up when they bought the place. As he set the food on the counter, it hit him that this was his first houseguest, outside his brothers. He pulled down two plastic plates and a couple of napkins. "Are you okay drinking beer from the bottle?"

"I don't drink it any other way." She leaned against the wood stall. "So, this is the kitchen." She pointed to the small sofa in the corner in front of a small television. "And the family room?"

"I have a sitting area in my bedroom with a comfy lounge chair and another TV. And then there is my office, where I suspect I'll spend most of my time when I'm not at my actual office."

"I still don't get why you don't all live in the house. I haven't been inside it in years. But from what I remember, it's huge. Plenty of room for all of you." She took her food and beer and plopped herself down on the sofa, kicking off her boots and resting her feet on his coffee table.

If one could call the piece of wood that he slapped four large sticks under a coffee table.

He hoped it didn't break. All he used it for was the remote, a few magazines, and maybe a drink. Never his feet. Of course, he'd lived in this stable all of a couple of days. And only slept in it one night.

"We've never all lived together before." He sat on the opposite end of the love seat. He had never understood why this size sofa had been named that until this moment. He wished he'd chosen to stand. He shifted before taking a healthy swig of his beer.

He should have brought the entire six-pack instead of putting the other four into the fridge.

"You're brothers. How is that possible?"

This was always so complicated to explain, but fun. "Seth, Trent, and I have one mother. Marcus, the baby, is the product of our father's second marriage. And Heath, the second oldest we didn't know about until he showed up at our doorstep when he was sixteen."

"Didn't you all live together then?"

"Seth had already left for the military when we learned of our father's affair with Heath's mom. He stayed with us for only a couple of years and they were difficult at best." Troy stared at her mouth, specifically her plump lips as she nibbled her pizza. He should shift his gaze, but he feared he'd only be able to lower it, which would be way worse.

"Why?"

"That's not my story to tell," he said. "Except for my dad didn't make it easy for Heath, who was an innocent boy who simply wanted to get to know his father and his brothers. So, a couple of years after Heath showed up, he left. I stayed in touch with him, but it was a struggle for my other brothers at times. Especially Seth because they had barely spent any time together and Seth resented my dad for cheating on our mom."

"I can't say as I blame him. That's a betrayal of a different kind, especially since I get the sense that you all were mama's boys."

Troy laughed. "Oh, we were. At least I'm told we were. As I've said, I don't remember her that much."

Esme shifted, tucking one foot under her butt. "Would you mind telling me what you do remember?"

Troy rubbed his chin. No one had ever asked him these kinds of questions before. He found them endearing. "I've got a sensitive nose and I remember how people smell. It sticks with me and my mother always smelled like a strawberry field."

Esme's mouth curved into a seductive smile. "How do I smell?"

"Like peaches and cream. Actually, more like peach cobbler."

"I use a peach-scented soap, though sometimes I like to change it up with mango," Esme said. "What else about your mom do you remember?"

He polished off his pizza while he sorted through the fuzzy memories that floated through his mind like gray clouds that collided in the sky, threatening to dump massive amounts of rain on the earth below, but never does. He searched for a clearer picture, one he could put into words. "She used to read to Trent and me from this big book. We would get so excited when she pulled out the massive storybook. We'd each get to pick one. Trent always picked *The Three Billy Goats Gruff* and I would have her read *The Little Engine That Could.*"

"Those are great choices."

"When she died, the entire vibe of the house changed. We were always a tad afraid of our father. Not in a bad way. He never hurt us or anything, but he was strict. After Mom passed, he became uncaring. Sometimes he could be mean in the name of teaching us to be men. The hardest part was always how he treated other young boys, as if they were his own and we were the interlopers. If a neighborhood kid showed interest in being a firefighter, he'd take that boy or girl under his wing and teach them everything he knew. But he never did that for us. Not even when I stuck it out and stayed home when I turned eighteen."

"Why'd you do that?" she asked.

His belly soured like a carton of milk left out in the sun. That was never an easy question to answer. "In part because I didn't want Marcus to be alone. He was only twelve and he missed his mom so much. He also missed Heath. He didn't understand why he had left. He was too young. I couldn't ask Trent to stay just because I was and while Trent begged me to go with him into the Air Force, he understood why I couldn't up and leave."

"Do you always care for everyone else before taking care of yourself?"

That was one reason Darlene had given for leaving him at the altar. She had told him later when she called that she'd become tired of not only being last in his life after his brothers and a father who didn't give a shit, but that he couldn't, or wouldn't, even put himself ahead of anyone. She told him it had become evident when he wanted to put on pause getting married and having a baby for a few years to give Heath and Seth a chance to mend their relationship.

She'd gotten pregnant anyway.

Or so Troy had thought. That's why he'd been so heartbroken when she left him.

"For the record, taking care of my brothers is

taking care of myself." He hadn't meant to sound so defensive. He stood, tossing his empty bottle in the recycle bin. He snagged two more beers from the fridge, opening them both. He set hers down on the coffee table. "I've only ever wanted one thing in life."

"What's that?"

"Family."

"Do you mean a wife and kids?"

He leaned against the windowsill. He walked right into that one without even trying. He was a shitty liar, but this was a part of his life he wasn't prepared to share. Anger still filled his heart. Darlene hadn't broken it. That would imply it could be mended.

She utterly crushed it.

While she hadn't left him void of emotion and he had real feelings for all the women he dated, he didn't find himself capable of total trust. Paranoia always seeped into his relationships like smoke dancing above a fire. It was inevitable.

The worst part was that he knew he was the problem. He understood he could change the narrative. He just didn't know how.

"Family comes in all sorts of shapes and sizes. But ever since Heath walked in and out of my life, I became determined to bring my brothers together where my father failed."

"I'd say you've done a good job of that, but that still doesn't explain why you're not all living under the same roof, unless you're all setting up for families."

He tossed his head back and laughed. There was a certain irony in that statement considering he'd already had that conversation with Marcus. "I can see my baby brother settling down, though not anytime soon. Maybe Seth. Trent? Not likely for the long haul and Heath likes the great outdoors more than he does people." He lowered his chin. "We live like this because as much as we want to be close to one another, we don't know how to share space. We've all been on our own for so long that we need boundaries." He raised his free hand. "This is the best of all worlds and if someone happens to—God forbid—fall in love, well, we can accommodate."

She raised both brows. "It would take a special woman to live with all of you."

"I think for now, we're all focused on settling into our new roles with the fire department here in Fool's Gold as well as with the Brotherhood Protectors. Finding a partner of the opposite sex isn't on our radar." He wished he could tear his gaze away, but instead he let himself get sucked into her deep, sensitive blue pools of sweetness.

It was like staring into the crashing waves of the ocean. It soothed his aching soul. The connection he felt for her swirled around in his gut, making its way into all aspects of his system. He wondered if she sensed it too, but it would be crazy to ask, so he opted for a different set of questions. "What about you? Any hopes of finding a husband and having babies?"

"My father would have loved me to do that, but I've always struggled in my dating life."

"I don't believe that." He pushed from the window. Sitting on the sofa with her was a mistake and he knew it, but he had no control over the pull she had. It was like the positive and negative ends of a magnet snapping together.

It was inevitable and he feared that before the night's end, he might make a move if something didn't stop him.

"You're beautiful. You're intelligent. I can't imagine anyone not wanting to spend time with you, much less not falling madly in love with you."

"You're a sweet man and from what I've learned in the short time I've known you, you're incredibly kind. You also have a way of making people feel comfortable."

"Not the first time I've been told that, but if you ask Darlene, my ex-fiancée, I was a real bastard."

"I'm sure Billy has a few choice words to describe me."

"I've got a few words to describe him." Troy raised his arm across the back of the sofa. "Manipulator would be one."

"You also owe me an explanation on why you

didn't tell me about the paper you found in my father's office with his plans to fire him."

"I'm going to answer that with a question."

She wiped her fingers with the napkin, pushed her plate across the coffee table, and took a long swig of her fresh beer. "I hate it when people do that."

He had to admit, he did too. But in this case, he felt it was reasonable. "Do you think it's possible your father could have been on the fence about firing Billy and that's why the paperwork wasn't attached to his file and all I found was a sticky note?"

"Absolutely." Esme tucked both feet under her butt, pressing her knees against his thighs.

His thoughts went right to what it would be like to hold her in his arms. He shouldn't assume that their physical contact meant anything since the sofa was so small and their bodies touching wasn't something unexpected.

But it could have been avoided if she had picked a different position.

"My dad had always been about protocol and safety. He liked rules."

"I think I would have liked your father." Troy took a couple of strands of her silky hair between his fingers. It sizzled his skin and sent his heart racing. "But as an outsider, looking at Billy's record on paper, he should have been fired a few years ago."

"While my father preached how important it was to follow every protocol we had as firefighters, he also whispered in all our ears that occasionally, gut instinct trumped everything. But instincts weren't always truths and it took years to hone which were the ones to follow and which were the ones to push to the side. He believed Billy had good instincts and knew how to use them. That's why he didn't fire him."

Troy had worked with a few men like Billy when he'd first started, but that kind of attitude would have never been accepted in the Air Force with his Fire Protection team. Going rogue was never an option.

People died when that happened.

"Other than Ashley, your father's assistant—now mine—who would have access to Billy's file?" Troy asked.

"Billy's captain."

"That would be Ashton Sullivan?"

"Correct, but I can see my dad keeping firing orders out of the file since Ashton and Billy are friends." Esme raised her hand and covered a yawn.

He glanced at the clock. It wasn't horribly late, but they did need to start early since they were driving to the prison to visit her mother in the morning.

That should prove to be interesting.

"Before we turn in for the night, I have two more questions for you." He polished off his beer, feeling the effects of the alcohol go straight to his brain. Knowing his mind wasn't functioning at full capacity, he dropped his hand to his lap. He couldn't afford to touch her hair, or any part of her any longer. He didn't trust he could stop.

"Shoot."

"Personally, I'm inclined to fire Billy. But I'm not sure that's a good look since one, I'm only acting fire chief, and two, I'm not sure what kind of message that sends to the rest of the department."

She pressed her finger over his mouth. "You already have the answer to this one."

"And what's that?"

She let out a short laugh. "To wait a week or so. Get a feel for your job and the people. Let Billy sweat. It won't be the first time."

"All right."

"So, what's the second question?"

"Who are your suspects because you and I both don't believe the fire that took your dad's life was an accident."

"I have no proof," she said.

"We have three firefighters who stated they saw that fire behaving as if there could have been accelerant."

"And yet we found none and no one smelled any." She stood, took the garbage off the table, and strolled across the kitchen, tossing it in the large bin by the opening that led to the rest of the stable. "Besides not thinking my mom would do this, I believe we're jumping the gun by visiting my mother."

"We're being proactive," Troy said.

She turned, planting her hands on her hips. "I've sent samples from every room in the house to an independent lab as well as the State lab. I have the medical examiner double-checking everything on my father's autopsy, which I'm hoping comes back tomorrow. Sparrow and one of my agents, the only one I trust, are going through the scene tomorrow, looking for anything we might have missed."

"Who is this agent?"

"His name is Colby Knott. He'll take over if I'm ever taken off the case. For that reason, I'm having him take an active role."

"That's smart." Troy would need to have a sit-down with this Colby guy. Troy trusted his judgment when it came to people and he knew the investigation was in good hands with Esme. However, her emotions were still a factor. This was her father. Her hero.

And the man who gave her a new destiny.

Her judgment could be skewed.

"The truth is, after looking through as much as I could so far from my dad's home office and thinking back on all our conversations, I'm at a loss for who could have done this and why." She waved her finger. "But the bigger problem is still, why did my dad go there in the first place? Why was he in that building? We'll know what we're looking for if we can answer that question."

He had to agree. "Let me show you to your quarters."

"You mean to my stable."

"That's funny." He pressed his hand on the small of her back and guided her down the center. "This is my office." He pointed to the door on his right. "I'll be staying there. I'll leave the door open slightly. The bathroom is behind that door and right here is my bedroom where you'll be staying." He slid open the barn door, showing off his king-size bed, with a bench he'd made himself for a footboard.

"Holy shit. I did not expect this." She turned and fell back on the bed. "This is amazing."

"I like it."

"I can't believe you pulled it together in only a few days."

"Us Falco boys are resourceful." He leaned over, pressing his hands on either side of her body, making sure he didn't slide onto the mattress, and kissed her temple. He stood. "I'll be in the next stable if you need me. The lights stay on in the main corridor, so keep the door closed if you like it dark. But don't go outside of this building, or you'll trip the alarm."

"Got it." She rolled. "Thanks for being one of the good guys."

He inwardly groaned. All the thoughts he'd been having about not leaving his bedroom evaporated. He'd do the right thing. The honorable thing.

"Good night, Esme."

CHAPTER 8

ESME STEPPED into the private visiting room the warden had arranged for the visit and shivered. Not only was it cold, but the mere idea of seeing her mother after all these years turned her blood to ice.

Ten years.

She sucked in a deep breath and counted backward from twenty before letting it out slowly. When she'd turned fifteen, she wanted to know where she came from and begged her father to allow her to visit her mom—Heather. Her dad hadn't been thrilled, but he made it happen under the caveat that Esme be willing to talk with a therapist.

She agreed and that had been the best decision she'd ever made since her visit had indeed been one of the most horrifying experiences Esme had ever had to live through and remember. Her mother hadn't even tried to be sweet or loving. No. She took one look at her fifteen-year-old daughter and said, *The devil lives inside you. I can help you cleanse your soul, but it will hurt.* She then went on to expose a secret Esme's father had kept from her from the day he pulled her from that fire.

How her mother knew about the connection to the family that Henri lost that day, Esme never asked.

And she never would.

Esme left the building ten minutes later. She didn't return again until she was twenty-three and that was only because her mother had begged. Curiosity had gotten the better of her good senses. The tone of the meeting had been entirely different. Her mom hadn't brought up any of her godly beliefs or thoughts on demons. However, she did have a lot to say about Esme's career choice.

Her mom was conflicted.

On the one hand, Heather believed Esme was doing God's work. She was helping rid the world of evil people.

Except there were some holy people who did things—like cleanse the world through fire—who were now rotting in prison.

And that had been the final rub. Her mother had wanted Esme to help her in her never-ending battles to appeal.

"Hey. Are you okay?" Troy asked as he tossed some files on the table. She'd driven so he could read up on her notorious mother. It had been a nerve-racking drive due to his silence. She had expected him to ask a million questions, but he kept his nose in the documents while she focused on things she shouldn't.

Last night, she had lain in his bed for a good thirty minutes, half expecting him to show up, knowing he wouldn't.

Phoebe, her stepmother, had described Esme's father as a dying breed. A real man's man. Meaning some would look at him and see this old-fashioned person and get the wrong impression. They'd mistake him for something he wasn't instead of understanding that being a gentleman, being chivalrous, had nothing to do with being in love with a feminist.

Esme saw her dad as living in the dark ages. He was strict, and while he took no issues with her ambitions in life and believed she could do and be anything she wanted, he did tell her that one of his dreams for his little girl was for her to have someone in her life who would take care of her. He wanted that to happen sooner rather than later so that as he aged, he wouldn't have to worry.

Phoebe told her that he wasn't being a chauvinist. Far from it. He wanted his daughter to find her person.

Sometimes Esme didn't understand Phoebe's philosophies on life, especially when it came to her dad. She was a bit of a free spirit. However, the more time she spent with Troy, the more she understood.

"I've met my mother twice. Neither time has been productive," she admitted.

He wrapped his arms around her, making her feel safe. "Your father was too close to the situation and so are you. There are deep emotions involved whether you want to admit it or not. I don't have the same ones. Maybe I can add a perspective that neither one of you can."

She tilted her head and stared into his eyes. Those damn caring, understanding eyes that made her want to lean into his strong body and let him take care of her forever.

Troy had to be one of the most respectful humans she'd ever met, yet his role was to protect her above all else. Most people in that position would tell her what to do and how to do it. That was often the nature of a protection detail. She had mentally prepared herself for friction regarding Troy and his job with the Brotherhood Protectors. She understood he had two different functions to perform.

One was as acting fire chief and the other was keeping her safe in case the fire hadn't been an accident.

Feeling vulnerable wasn't an emotion she handled well and she tended to rebel against anyone who tried to take care of her in times of crisis. That included her father. However, Troy made it easy to accept his help. He never stepped on her toes or made her feel like she had no choice.

The weirdest thing about that was she liked having Troy around, and she liked him. If Billy or any other man she dated tried to swoop in and be her knight in shining armor, she would have dug her heels in and told them to take a hike.

However, it did bother her that Troy kept her at arm's length. If she wanted Troy, she would have to make it clear and push him to understand that she accepted the kind of man he'd become.

He didn't have to spell it out. He was everything her father wanted for her except one thing and she could see it deep in his soul. As she pressed her hand against his chest, she could feel the pain that burned through his system.

Someone had taken a piece of his heart and blackened it.

Her father had been like that for years and she thought he'd never recover.

Troy tucked a few strands of her hair behind her ears. "What are you thinking about right now, because you've left the building."

Tears filled her eyes. She blinked, squeezing out two. "The fire my dad saved me from killed his fiancée and she'd been pregnant."

"Jesus," Troy whispered.

"My dad hadn't told me because he always

worried I'd feel like I was some kind of replacement for them, which I know I wasn't."

"How did you find out?"

She glanced over her shoulder at the door her mom would soon be walking through.

"Your mother? You've got to be kidding me," Troy said. "How did she find out? When did she tell you? And I hope you weren't too mad at your dad. He was just trying to protect your feelings. And your relationship."

Esme broke the embrace. It felt too comfortable. Too caring. Too easy. She sat in the hard metal chair, pulling her sweater tight. "I was fifteen. I'm sure she had no idea if I knew or not and she enjoyed hurting me. I could tell by the way she smiled and stared at me."

"I can do this interview alone." Troy knelt in front of her, taking her hands. "You don't have to put yourself through this kind of torture. It's not necessary."

"I'm fine." She blew out a puff of air. "I deal with Heather's cruel letters and I've learned it has nothing to do with me. To answer your earlier question, I was angry with my dad for not telling me, but only because I sometimes saw him sitting in his office, staring at a picture, holding a glass of scotch, crying. I didn't understand it. And he'd clam up when I'd ask him. Things got better when he married Phoebe, but still, I didn't know who the woman in the picture was or why it hurt my dad so much. Phoebe told me that sometimes parents had pains that had nothing to do with their kids and when he was ready, he'd share with me."

"That's a nonanswer, but it wasn't her place to tell you anything."

Esme nodded. "Heather destroyed many lives during her reign as the Colorado Firestarter." She squared her shoulders. The scars on her body tightened. "When I came back here the second time, I enjoyed telling her that I would forever give statements to the courts that she should not ever be up for parole or given a new trial. I know who Heather Roman is, and while she and I might share DNA, that doesn't make me anything like her."

"If you want to pause or end the interview, you just say the word." He palmed her cheek. "I read some of the letters you gave me from Heather and I'm a little surprised you continue to open them."

"I've always worried that she'll come after me. That she'll try to finish what she started." Saying those words out loud to anyone other than her dad felt strange. No. They horrified her to the depths of her core.

"And your dad? Was that something that concerned him as well?"

"It was something that was always in the back of his mind. We have kept a finger on the pulse of her cultlike following. It's a small group, and we know they haven't ever set a fire, but they constantly preach about how important it is to destroy the demons in our society."

"Do you believe your dad was always honest with you about his discussions with Heather when he came to visit?"

"I did until he didn't tell me about Chuck Manzo," she said. "He always believed knowledge was power and if he thought Heather was up to her old tricks, he'd want me to be protected. This is why I struggle to believe she could be behind his death or why he was acting weird. If he thought she was involved in anything, he'd be demanding I stay with him or he'd have Stone and Sparrow involved."

"All right," Troy said. "What about exorcisms? Is that something these groups are doing?"

"Not in years," she said. "Everything I have, all the newspaper clippings, the letters, anything of relevance related to Heather Roman and her following, I gave to you."

He ran his thumb under her eye. His mouth was so close to hers that she could taste the cinnamon roll he had for breakfast. Slowly, he leaned closer until the warmth of his lips pressing firmly against hers stole her breath.

She gripped his shoulders for support as his tongue found hers, twisting and twirling in an uncharted dance.

The sound of metal rattling echoed in her ears.

He jerked his head. "Bad timing. I'm sorry." He stood, stuffing his hands in his pockets.

She wiped her lips and swirled, facing the door. As it swung open, it made a screeching noise, almost like fingers scraping against a chalkboard.

A guard stepped into the room, followed by her mother in shackles, then another guard.

"What have we here," her mother said in a singsong voice. "Have you come to tell me you're getting married? Or are you already and I'm going to be a grandmother?"

Esme swallowed the bile that had bubbled up her throat. "I'm sure you heard that my dad died in a fire the other day."

Her mom—or Heather—tilted her head. "That man was not your father. I don't know why you insist on calling him that." Heather took a seat across from Esme.

The guard adjusted the shackles, locking them against the chains on the table.

"Of course, your real daddy wasn't any better. He was a weak man, allowing the devil into his soul." Heather leaned forward. "Much like you."

In the past, Esme might engage in this discussion for a moment or two, trying to understand what made Heather tick. But right now, they had a list of things they needed to get through and Heather often tried to redirect to accomplish her own agenda.

Whatever that was.

"What can you tell us about Chuck Manzo?" Esme asked.

"I'm sure you know more about him than I do." Heather glanced between Esme and Troy. "However, I'm happy to give you my impression of the man once you tell me who this fine specimen of a man is and what he means to you."

"I don't mean anything to Esme," Troy said. "I'm the new fire chief."

Ouch. But he was wise to play it that way.

"Now answer the question, please." Troy folded his arms across his chest and glared.

Damn. That was a side of him Esme hadn't expected. Mr. Honest-Troy-Falco had turned into an intimidating, hard-hitting bad cop investigator.

Heather leaned back and smiled. Her eyes danced like the devil. "What's your name, Fire Chief?"

"Troy Falco."

"Wait a second. I know that name." Heather glanced toward the ceiling. She tapped her finger against the metal tabletop.

Esme cringed. Heather was trying to get under Troy's skin. She was the master manipulator. She was good at reading people and finding their weaknesses. Once she did, she exploited it.

"I don't see how," Troy said.

Heather shook her head. "No. The name Falco is ringing bell after bell after bell. Maybe I knew your mama." She leaned forward. "Or your daddy."

"Highly unlikely," Troy said. "They're both dead and they didn't die in a fire that you started. And I don't see where you might have come across them."

"That doesn't mean I don't know them." She winked.

"We'd have to be from around here, and we're not. Now, can we please stop playing games. We have a fire to investigate and jobs to do and I don't like having my time wasted."

Esme watched as her mother's eyes narrowed and she drew her lips together into a tight line.

Heather did not like to lose and she just got shut down, big-time.

"We need to know about Chuck Manzo and if he could have started the fire that killed Esme's father," Troy said. "Or if you ordered it."

"I'm not some mafia queen." Heather glared. "Anything I do is commanded by God and as I've told everyone in here, as well as my lawyers and anyone else who will listen, I know I was misguided in my actions when I set those fires. I misunderstood my callings. I'm trying to change that. But some people still misunderstand my intentions."

Esme was so tired of the way her mom tried to change the rhetoric so she could be absolved of her crimes. "You've said many times that all those people were meant to perish."

"The demons were meant to be banished." Heather waggled her finger. "There is a difference my child. It's not my fault that humans chose the devil over our dear Lord."

Chills crawled across Esme's skin.

"I'm learning to understand the way God communicates to me." She glanced around the small room. "Even this incarceration is a gift from God." She smiled. "It's not a punishment, though I know I wasn't meant to be here for life. God has forgiven me of my sin. Society needs to do the same. I have much good work to complete, and the devil is rampant in our world."

"Does your work include finishing what you started? With me?" Esme hadn't meant to ask the question, but the moment it left her lips, she braced herself for impact.

"I never wanted to hurt you," Heather said. "I only wanted the evil spirits to leave you. That's my calling. Not just to help you with them. But all of mankind. It's my purpose in life. Only the man you called father continually poisoned you and now you choose—"

"We don't have time for this," Troy said. "You haven't answered anything about Chuck Manzo. We need to circle back to that."

"He's been told many times that the proper way to banish a demon is through proper channels and he doesn't have the training. Not yet anyway," Heather said.

"Training?" Troy asked.

Heather nodded. "Yes. God has commanded me to learn the correct techniques and I have told Chuck he can too."

"Where? A school? Online? Be specific," Esme said.

"I recommended some books and there are online classes. When I get out, I intend to offer spiritual guidance for family members living with loved ones possessed by the demonic and needing help casting them out." Once again Heather smiled that creepy smile that made Esme want to run for the hills. "See. I've grown and changed since the last time we chatted."

Esme wouldn't go that far. All she'd done was become a better manipulator to get what she wanted.

Out of prison and back to where she could go on a murdering rampage.

"Would he, or any of your other followers, take it upon themselves to kill Henri Jade?" Troy asked.

She lifted her gaze. She wouldn't have worded that question that way, much less asked it because what would be the point. They weren't getting anywhere.

"Chuck, absolutely not. He wants to do right by God. He's a good soldier. As for some of the others, I don't know. There are a few I have stopped corresponding with because they aren't true believers. They want fame, fortune, or to be associated with me, and that's not what this is about."

Troy inched closer to the table and sat down, his demeanor slightly more relaxed, but still quite serious. "How do you know when someone is faithful and someone is full of shit?"

"You're not a man of faith and it shows. Same with my daughter. But Henri was and he would come in here and try to trick me. Others have tried to use my faith against me. I do the same thing, but for different reasons." She shrugged. "I have to know if those who are going to join me will be true to my calling, or will they end up misreading, misinterpreting God's word. Or worse, using it for something else."

"Like you did," Esme said under her breath.

Heather sighed. "That's not what happened. Everyone who died in those fires was possessed and had done bad things. They were prostitutes. Drug addicts. Criminals. And they also chose to stay with their demons. I will admit now that I've had many conversations with my higher power that I misread what the Lord commanded me to do, but God was still going to take those men and women whether I started those fires or not."

"And what about me? You left me in that building to die." Esme's skin prickled with heat. "I was a child. How was I supposed to understand some divine power or choice or whatever bullshit you're spewing today?"

"No, sweetheart. I left you there to be saved. But

you always choose to forget that part of the story and focus on the lies Henri fed you." Heather tapped her finger against the table. She glanced over her shoulder. "Guard, I think we're done here."

"I've got a couple more questions," Troy said.

"Like what?" Heather tilted her head as if she were intrigued, but Esme knew better. It was all for show.

"For starters, what did you and Fire Chief Jade discuss at his last visit?"

Heather narrowed her stare. "I'm not sure that's any of your business."

"We differ on that point," Troy said. "I'd appreciate it if you would humor me."

"If you must know, he came to ask me the same bullshit questions he always does and he made a request." Heather held Esme's gaze. "He wanted me to stop corresponding with my daughter. I told him that would never happen. Now, if you don't mind, I'd like to go because it's time for my favorite talk show."

The guard shifted his gaze between Troy and Esme.

"We're done," Esme said.

Troy nodded.

It took the guards three minutes to escort Heather out of the room.

"I knew she wouldn't be straightforward, but thanks for everything you said and did." Esme stood, taking Troy's hand. "It's hard to believe she's my mother."

"It's just biology." He kissed her softly. "I texted forensics to see where we are at with the report. They said by the end of the day. Tomorrow at the latest."

"We can't talk to Chuck unless we have signs of arson. Otherwise, we've got no case."

"How do you feel about helping me go through your dad's work office this afternoon? His computer, all his files, everything. Maybe we'll stumble onto something that will give us direction."

"I love that idea. Thank you." She pressed her hand against his chest. "But you can't kiss me in that office. I'll be taken off this case so fast it will make both our heads spin."

"I have a sudden urge to watch *The Exorcism.*"

"You have an inappropriate sense of humor and I adore you for it." She raised up on tiptoe and kissed his cheek. "How about we do a double feature tonight and toss in *The Omen.*"

"You seriously like those kinds of movies?"

"As long as it doesn't have a clown, we're good."

He laughed, taking her hand and tugging her toward the door. "I'm in trouble with a capital *T.*"

AFTER TURNING on the blinker of Troy's truck, Esme glanced in the rearview mirror. She eased onto the highway. "Not a bad ride," she said.

"I like it." Troy glanced up from his paperwork. "Thanks for driving. I wasn't prepared for all the paperwork I'd have to deal with between my two jobs, but you're giving me a chance to get caught up."

"Not a problem. It gives me something to focus on after visiting Heather." Esme hadn't expected to feel anything toward her birth mother except maybe anger and disgust. Those two emotions lingered in her system, but they weren't the driving force of her heart. No. She felt a sense of sadness and loss. Grief had overwhelmed her soul and she had nowhere to file it. "It always bothered my dad that I read her letters."

"Why do you?"

Her father always told her that her questions would never be answered. That the letters were Heather's way of keeping Esme in her life in the hopes of having her feel pity so she'd give her a hand with the prison system and her lawyers. But with every letter came an ounce of hope. Deep down, Esme knew her dad was right, but she couldn't let go of the need to understand and her father didn't know what it was like to be her any more than she understood his pain.

"The first time I visited Heather, who claimed to love me, I asked her to explain how a mother could leave a child in a burning building to die. I told her I wanted to know how that made sense in the eyes of God. I got a lot of bullshit about demons, and I told her when she was ready to tell me the truth, she could write me."

"You opened yourself up to a lot of communication."

"That's what my dad told me." Esme checked her mirrors and noticed a fancy sport SUV racing up on her left about ten cars behind. Whoever was driving zipped to the right, crossed three lanes, and moved up two cars. She gripped the steering wheel with both hands. She had been driving SUVs her entire life, and she'd handled a fire engine just fine when she worked as a firefighter, but she was doing seventy miles an hour, in heavy traffic, with an asshole weaving in and out, heading right for her.

That made her uncomfortable.

"For a long time, I worried there was a piece of her inside me, so I looked for that in those letters."

"Did you ever find it?" Troy set his hands on top of his papers and kept his gaze fixated on her, something she valued in his personality. It made her feel important and that wasn't something she'd gotten from a lot of men in her life lately.

"No. And for that reason, I'm glad she wrote the letters and that I read them. It helped me see that there is more of my dad in me than any other human out there. Biology isn't necessary. Love is."

Troy reached out and squeezed her thigh.

"Shit," she mumbled.

The vehicle came right up behind her, nearly

tapping the back of Troy's truck, then swerved to her blind side. She couldn't move to her left because another car was there, but she could slow, so she tapped the brakes.

"Hold on," she said.

"What is this asshole doing?"

"He's going to kill someone."

Suddenly, the SUV cut in front of her, clipping the front end of the pickup. She skidded to the right, barely avoiding two cars.

Horns honked.

Cars whizzed by, avoiding hitting her as she eased off the road. Once she was sure the vehicle was far enough to the side, she put it in park. "I didn't get a plate number."

Troy had his cell in his hand. "Neither did I, but I'm calling Sparrow anyway with a description." He glanced up. "We go visit your mom, and then we get run off the road? That's something to investigate."

Esme had to agree.

CHAPTER 9

TROY CONTINUED to rifle through Henri's files. He kept meticulous notes, even handwritten ones. Better than Troy, which was impressive because Troy would rewrite his notes if he made a mistake. Troy's brothers, especially Trent, constantly picked on Troy for his obsessive nature. As small children, Trent would hide all of Troy's color-coded pencils and pens. Trent thought it was hysterical, but it made Troy's skin itch. Troy had a need for organization, and taking over this office had been pure joy.

Except for one thing.

Henri had to die in order for Troy to get there and it broke Esme's heart. He glanced at the beautiful woman sitting behind his desk. His brothers would be off tonight and he contemplated which one he'd talk to about the emotions that stirred in his system. He'd been in love before and he knew what that felt like. He understood how it could come out of nowhere when you least expected it, hitting you like a twister that dropped down from the sky, sucking you in, and then spitting you out like unwanted debris.

Shit. Darlene had done such a number on him that anytime he had feelings for a woman, all he could think about was being left on the pavement like roadkill. He called himself a runner when it came to relationships. He desired companionship. Human touch. But the moment it got too real, he turned into someone else and made sure his heart was protected.

Esme had already wormed her way into the fabric of his being and he hadn't even slept with her yet. He barely knew her, but he couldn't imagine not having her in his life.

It was madness and he didn't know which one of his brothers might understand.

Marcus was still so young. At twenty-six, he might have seen the world through the military and had some experiences most men his age haven't had. But when it came to women, he wasn't the one Troy should be talking to.

Seth was a smart man. Experienced. Seasoned. But he had issues and was currently focused on one woman he thought had an affair with their father, who didn't, but there was no talking to Seth about it.

Heath was a loner. What the hell did he know?

That left his twin, Trent.

Who would probably break out that damn Ouija board and ask the spirits while poking massive amounts of fun at Troy. However, the one thing Troy could count on when it came to Trent was that of all his brothers, Trent had felt what Darlene had done to him.

The twin connection.

"How's it going with your father's computer?" Troy asked.

"Nothing out of the ordinary," Esme said. "I'm copying anything I think we might need to take a closer look at pertaining to my mother onto a hard drive."

"I want you to also copy anything with Billy or Micky's name and anyone else who has been suspended multiple times."

She lifted her gaze. "Why are you so hot for Billy?"

"He is kind of handsome, but not my type."

"That's not what I meant." She shook her head. "I know he's a bit much, but my dad kept him on for a reason. I trust my father's judgment. You should too."

"I do, but you saw that sticky note and agreed it was your father's handwriting. So, why did your father have exit papers drawn up, then put a hold on them, and why can't we find them?"

She nodded. "All right. I'll agree that is cause for concern."

Troy continued to set aside the closed files

regarding the Colorado Firestarter along with anything he thought might be remotely related. He stuck his head out the door. "Hey, Ashley, can you come here and make copies for me?"

"Sure thing, boss," Ashley called from down the hall. A few seconds later, she popped into the office. "Oh, hey, Esme. How are you doing?"

"No worse for wear." Esme smiled, leaning back in the chair. "How are those babies?"

"Still keeping me up at night." Ashley sighed. "Everyone says they will start sleeping through the night soon, but people forget I have twins. One wakes up at two in the morning, and the other wakes up at three. It's not fun."

"I have a twin brother," Troy said. "According to my older brother, once my parents put us in different rooms, we stopped waking each other up."

"Really? Everyone tells me I shouldn't separate them since they are only three months old and they spent nine months in the womb together."

"Yeah, that's the norm philosophy, and once we were two, we started climbing out of our cribs or beds and started sleeping together again, but as infants, our crying woke the other up. Or so my brother says." Troy plopped a couple more files on the desk.

"I'm going to give that a try," Ashley said. "You know, I can put all these on a hard drive to save paper."

"That works." Troy nodded. "But I want a hard copy of the Colorado Firestarter file."

Ashley lifted the pile. "Do you mind if I ask why? Especially when you've got an expert sitting right here."

"I want to be able to mark them up with my own notes. It helps me organize and think about things from a different perspective."

"What about Chief Jade's copies?" Ashley asked.

Troy stole a glance at Esme. "I haven't seen any. Have you?"

"No," Esme said. "I'm not surprised he kept a hard copy, but I am surprised we haven't seen it. I've been through his home office and now this one."

Thankfully, Esme didn't mention anything about her father's home being broken into. While Ashley was on the list of people he could trust, both from the Brotherhood Protectors and from Esme, the fewer people who knew about the breach, the better.

"Where does he usually keep them?" Troy asked.

"He has a special file. It's labeled Heather Roman, Personal. I'm not exactly sure where he keeps it. I just know that I make the copy and gave it to him," Ashley said.

"When did my dad have the copy made?" Esme asked.

"The last time he visited Heather," Ashley said.

"That was right before his death." Troy leaned

against the desk. "Did he tell you what the nature of that visit was? Or did he mention anything about it?"

"Boy. You like to rapid fire questions," Ashley said. "He goes there once a year. However, it's never an official visit and this was the first time in the eight years I've worked here that he's asked me to make a copy of Heather Roman's file." She held up her hand. "I didn't question it. I didn't believe it was my place."

The warden's record of the visit had been personal, as every other visit had been.

"I know I've asked this before, but I'm going to rephrase the parameters." Esme closed the laptop. "Since my father came back from visiting Heather, what was his demeanor like?"

"He's been off for a month, so it started before he went there." Ashley shifted the files in her arms. "When he came back, he asked me to refile every-thing in the archives. I did as I was asked and I didn't question him on the visit. He's always been emotional when it came to Heather."

Troy exhaled. "Thanks, Ashley. If you think of anything that you believe might be unusual, please don't hesitate to reach out, day or night."

She nodded and took two steps into the hallway and turned. "My husband told me something that has been bothering me."

"What's that?" Esme asked.

"Your father has never been one to gamble, but

my hubby has seen him at the casino three times in the two weeks before his death," Ashley said.

"Was he with anyone?" Troy asked.

"My husband saw him lurking in the shadows. He didn't stay long," Ashley said. "Sorry. I will see if I can get more information."

"Thanks, but if you wouldn't mind, could you have your husband contact me directly?" Troy asked.

"Sure. His name is Dereck. He works at the casino. He'll be there all night." Ashley disappeared down the hallway.

"What do you make of that?" Troy asked.

Esme leaned back in the big leather chair and swiveled left and right. "I don't know. Sparrow's dad spends a fair amount of time at the casino, so if my dad had been hanging around, I think I would have heard, but Dereck wouldn't lie about something like that. But what bothers me is Ashley's choice of words."

"You mean saying your dad was lurking."

Esme nodded. "It implies he was possibly doing undercover work, which is out of the scope of his job description."

"That is true. The only reason I'm helping is because of my role with the Brotherhood Protectors."

"I think we should go to the casino tonight," Esme said.

"Maybe Stone and Sparrow can meet us?"

"I happen to know they have dinner plans with Clint and Avery."

"Clint works for the Brotherhood Protectors. I met him when I stopped in the office. Why don't we see if they can all join us?" Troy asked.

She pulled out her cell and tapped on the screen. "I'll text them now."

"Good," he said.

"Oh. That was quick." She set her cell on the desk. "It's all set, but it's going to look an awful lot like we're on a date and Fool's Gold is a small town."

"Would that be so bad?" He arched a brow and lifted the corner of his mouth into a half smile.

"It could get you fired."

Oh, how he loved sparring with her. It was absolutely intoxicating. If he wasn't in this office, he'd lift her butt right out of that chair and kiss her until she went weak in the knees.

Or he did.

Or both.

"I don't think so," he mused. "Your boss is the fire marshal. I'm in an entirely different chain of command. Fraternizing rules don't apply."

"I think the Brotherhood Protectors have procedures in place about being entangled with those you're employed to protect."

"Did you hire me?"

She bit her lower lip and shook her head. "I believe you're doing this is a courtesy of some kind."

"I don't see a problem for us to go on a date, or anything else for that matter."

He leaned forward and took her hand, pressing his lips against her skin. His body ignited like the gas being turned all the way up when pilot light switch was flipped. "Why don't we head back to my place as soon as Ashley comes back with those files so we can get ready for our date."

"We have a few hours."

He leaned closer. "I know," he whispered.

ESME LEANED against the doorway to Troy's bedroom and stared deep into his intense eyes. During the entire ride from the county office to Paradise Ranch, they discussed the case and what little they had to go on.

The autopsy had been delayed, but they should get that tomorrow.

The reports on the fire were still at the independent lab. They could still come in by the end of the day, but there was nothing they could do until that happened.

As of this moment, the fire still looked like an accident, and they were no closer to finding out why her dad had been in that building in the first place.

"You're incredibly sexy when you're thinking about work." Troy kissed her neck. His hands rested on her hips, just under her shirt. His thumbs found her bare skin.

"How do you know that's where my mind was?"

"Because your right eye narrows slightly when your brain is going a mile a minute." He ran his fingers through her hair, cupping the back of her neck. "But when you're fully focused on something else, the muscles in your face relax a bit and your eye stops shifting."

She licked her lips. Her chest rose up and down as she tried to take in a deep breath.

His lips went from her neck to her cheek to her lips. His kisses were soft and tender. Gentle and sweet. "I want you to know that I'm not going to stop until we find out what happened to your father."

He held her face with both hands. His stare was so heartfelt she crumpled into his arms.

She tugged desperately at his clothes, needing to feel their naked bodies against one another. She didn't want to savor the moment. She didn't want to take it slow. She wanted hard and uncontrollable. Something wild in nature, but still passionate and respectful.

If that made any sense.

Never had she been with a man who allowed her this kind of raw energy. He let her take the lead as they tossed their shirts and pants to the side, falling onto the bed without a care in the world.

She gasped, pressing her hand against the center

of his chest. "Protection," she managed to say. "Do you have any? Because I'm not on birth control."

"I do." He reached across her body and opened the nightstand drawer, pulling out a small box of condoms.

"If I had gone snooping last night, I would have found those, huh?"

"Yes, you would have." He opened the box, pulling one out and setting it aside. "I wasn't a Boy Scout, but one does have to be prepared."

She laughed. "I should have suggested we stop on the way back."

"And I would have said I have some at home." He kissed her nose. "Now, can we stop talking?" He ran his hand up her stomach and cupped her breast, fanning her nipple.

She arched her back and moaned. "As long as you keep doing that."

"What about this?" His hand slid up between her legs.

"That works." She took in slow, shallow breaths and closed her eyes, losing herself in all the sensations that his touch created. All the nerve endings in her body exploded like firecrackers. His hands and mouth were everywhere, not letting a single inch go untouched.

He teased and tortured her, bringing her close to the edge, but not letting her go over. Every time she reached for him, or tried to do the same, he batted her hands away. He made her the center of attention. It was as if she was the only one that mattered.

That her pleasure was more important than anything else.

No one had ever treated her that way before. Sure, she'd had attentive lovers before who cared about making sure she was satisfied.

But this went above and beyond the call of duty.

Troy put her on a pedestal. He made her feel valued. Cared for.

Loved.

She shuddered as her climax began to build. Her toes curled as she dug her fingers into his scalp. A slow burn rolled across her skin. "Yes," she whispered. A fire filled her veins. Her orgasm tore through her system. It hit her hard and fast. She never experienced anything like it and she didn't want it to end.

He kissed his way up her midriff, stopping for a moment at her chest, toying with her nipples, making her climax linger even longer.

Reaching across the bed, he found the condom and ripped it open.

Her body tingled in anticipation.

A sense of selfishness filled her mind. She should be taking the time to explore his body, but all she could think about was him inside her, rocking her world again.

And that's exactly what he did.

It was as if they climbed on a rocket ship, fired up the engines, and took off at light speed for the moon. Her body quivered for what seemed like forever. She dug her fingernails into his back and wrapped her legs around his body, drawing him in as far as possible and holding him until his orgasm spilled over. It was the most magical thing that had ever happened.

He ruined her sexually for any other man.

There would never be anyone who could please her the way Troy did and she didn't want anyone to.

That thought got stuck in the middle of her throat.

She squeezed her eyes closed. There was no way she could be falling for Troy. Not that quick. It didn't matter that she watched Stone and Sparrow fall in love in weeks.

That was different.

Esme didn't love.

Not because she wasn't capable. But because she didn't trust enough to allow a man into her heart.

How the hell had Troy landed in the center of her soul?

"You're so beautiful," he whispered as he kissed her neck, lulling her into the present. "And intelligent and wonderful and—"

She cupped his face. "You got me in bed. You can stop the flattery."

He kissed her nose and smiled. "I'm only saying

the truth." He rolled to the side, propping himself up on his elbow. "I've never met anyone quite like you."

"Normally men say these kinds of things during the seduction part of the dance."

He chuckled. "This isn't going to be sexy."

"All right," she said. "What do you mean by someone like me?"

"You're pragmatic."

"You're right. That's not a word that's going to get a woman to take her clothes off." She reached for the blanket and brought it haphazardly over her body, barely covering her breasts. It wasn't that she felt like she needed to cover herself up, but there was a slight chill in the air.

"I'm wired differently. I find being realistic about things to be a total turn-on."

"That does kind of make sense."

He tucked a few stray stands of hair behind her ear. "You approach things logically, without too much emotion, even when you're feeling everything under the sun." He flattened his hand on the center of her chest. "You're good at covering your feelings with most people and I feel honored that you've shared a lot of them with me."

"I don't trust easily and I'm finding myself wondering why I trust you so much."

"I'm in the same boat," he said. "I've had no desire to be in a relationship that has any depth to it since Darlene left me. My only goal in life had been to get my brothers together and for us to be a team. A family."

"You've done that."

"I didn't think I wanted anything beyond having my brothers at my side."

"What are you saying?"

"Hey, Troy. You in there?" a male voice asked.

She pushed herself to a sitting position, clutching the blanket.

"I'll be out in a second." Troy jumped to his feet and found his jeans. "That's Trent. I better go find out what he wants." Quickly, he checked his phone. "We need to leave in about forty-five minutes. I'll take Trent into the kitchen, so you can sneak into the bathroom."

"Thanks."

Troy slipped out into the stable, leaving her there to contemplate her feelings and the knowledge that if her father were still alive, he'd be begging her to keep Troy in her life.

TROY STEPPED into the main corridor of the stable, pulling a shirt over his head. His heart swelled. He'd brought his brothers together and he was proud of that fact. His brothers rallied because they wanted it too. They had been tired of how their father manipulated and put a wedge between all their relationships.

Team Falco, in a way, was a big fuck you to their father.

The second they all pulled into Paradise Ranch, Troy felt a sudden and profound sense of accomplishment.

But there was something missing, and he couldn't put his finger on it. He thought maybe it was because it was still so new and relationships with his brothers were still forming and growing.

However, holding Esme in his arms, he realized it was something else, and that fucking terrified him. He hadn't given being married or having a family a second thought after Darlene dumped him and now he questioned his entire life.

"Were you taking a nap in the middle of the day?" Trent asked with an all-knowing smirk plastered on his face.

Troy didn't answer. There was no point. He led his twin into the kitchen and offered him a beer.

Trent took it.

"What's up?" Troy asked as the pipes in the old stable rattled with water. Even if he wanted to deny he'd been with someone, he couldn't based on that.

"You slept with her," Trent said matter-of-factly. "That's taking a protection detail to new levels."

"You didn't come banging on my door to tell me that."

Trent laughed. "You like her. You really like her."

Troy took a swig of his beer. "Are we going to

stand here and poke fun at me all day, or are you going to tell me what you want?"

"Oh. We're going to do both, bro." Trent set his longneck on the counter and folded his arms. "Especially when you're this defensive about a woman you just met. You've got it bad. Like your heart in my chest bad." Trent tapped his chest. "I can feel it."

"You're about to feel my finger poke you in about three seconds if you don't get to the point."

Trent held his hands out. "Okay. Okay. I get you don't want to talk about it, but damn, bro. You haven't had real feelings for a woman in forever. Good for you."

Troy sucked in a deep breath. "I don't know if it's good or not, but I can't swallow because there's a thick lump in my throat all the time. Professionally, I just fucked up and personally, I'm in way over my head."

Trent reached out and squeezed his shoulder. "You're right where you need to be. Trust me."

Troy nodded. "Now that we got that out of the way. You're not here to shoot the shit."

"No. I'm not." Trent ran a hand through his hair. "We heard some chatter at the fire station that I'm not sure you've been made aware of and it has to do with Billy Rocha."

"What's that?"

"There was a fire sixteen years ago that took the lives of three high school students. All female. It was proven to be arson. Billy had been picked up for questioning regarding that fire along with Micky Glass and two other guys by the name of Brett McGraw and Andrew Kimber."

"What was the outcome?" The hair on the back of Troy's neck stood at attention.

"Billy, Micky, and Brett all had airtight alibis. Andrew did not. The police went after him with all they had, but that was all circumstantial and he was found not guilty. However, the town blamed him and basically ran him and his family out. He lives in Colorado Springs and works as a defense attorney."

Troy narrowed his stare. "Interesting choice of career. Either he wants to help people like him get off or—"

"He specializes in helping those who are already incarcerated for crimes they didn't commit. He's helped to prove eight cases in the last ten years," Trent said. "I looked him up and my gut says that man was set up sixteen years ago to take the fall for a fire he didn't set. I think you should go talk to him."

"First I need to talk to Esme." Troy immediately felt his twin's concern. It resonated in the pit of his stomach like sour milk. "Why shouldn't I discuss this with her?"

"I think she's a good person and my gut says she's the real deal. But she was dating Billy at the time and Billy helped point the finger at Andrew."

"I'm aware," Troy said. "We've talked at great

length about her past relationship. There is no love lost between them when it comes to that. She does tend to defend her father for keeping him on as a firefighter after being suspended so many times."

"So, there's some loyalty there that might be undeserving based on history."

Troy couldn't argue that point, so he didn't bother.

"I want you to think about the fact she didn't tell you about this fire, especially considering the fact that Billy was in the same building that her father died in and so was Micky."

"Is anyone at the station thinking Billy or Micky could have had anything to do with the chief's death?"

Trent shook his head. "But this Brett guy is back in town and they all find him to be a cocky son of a bitch. He was a popular guy in high school, but only because he was a bully. People still don't like him, but the weird thing is his presence is town is gossip. It's like someone thought they saw him, but no one is sure, and everyone thinks that's weird."

"Why?"

"Because Brett is flashy and likes attention. The last time he came home he threw himself a party, but I'm more concerned about the fact that Esme didn't tell you about the Smith fire and Billy's connection to it."

"All right. I need to think about this. Keep me posted."

"Will do." Trent nodded. He snagged his beer and strolled out of the stable.

Troy raced back to his bedroom and sent an email to his assistant, asking for the files regarding the fire that Billy had been questioned about. Then he texted Jim, the sheriff—not Sparrow—asking for their files. He didn't want Sparrow telling Esme what he was up to.

Not yet, anyway.

Wonderful.

Keeping things from Esme was not a good idea if he wanted a relationship with her, but what was he supposed to do when she hadn't thought enough to tell him about this part of Billy's past?

Especially when he was considering firing him.

CHAPTER 10

"THANKS FOR TAKING your break with me." Troy glanced around the casino as he took a seat in a corner booth not far from where Esme and the rest of the gang waited. He hated these places. The constant dinging of the slot machines rattled his brain, jumbling his thoughts. The incessant chatter of gamblers made it impossible to organize his surroundings.

"I'm happy to help," Dereck, his assistant's husband, said. "Although, I'm not sure I can shed any light on the situation."

"Ashley said you saw Henri Jade hanging around here shortly before he died."

"I did, and I have to say in all the years I've worked here, that was a first. I don't know Henri very well, but he took my wife and I out to dinner once a year. He always busted my ass about working here."

"Ashley told me that you didn't get a chance to talk to him when you noticed him." Troy stole a glance at Esme, who stared at him while she sipped her drink at the bar, waiting for the table with her friends. She had been seething when Troy mentioned he wanted to talk to Dereck alone. He'd been shocked when she gave up the fight so quickly, but Sparrow had helped him talk her into it, so he owed her one.

"We were short-staffed, so I was helping behind the bar. I noticed him hanging out in a corner booth. He was wearing a baseball cap. The chief never wore those. Ever. Not even at a baseball game. And he had on a sweatshirt. Henri was the kind of guy who still believed in ties. I wasn't even sure it was him, but he paid with a credit card."

"What did he do while he was here?"

"He had one drink and left. I was going to go over and talk to him, but he was gone before I got the chance."

"You didn't notice him talking to anyone?" Troy asked.

"No. But I thought that was odd too because Billy and Micky were here."

"Did you happen to pay attention to what they were doing?" Troy pulled out his cell and tapped the screen, finding a picture of Brett. "Were they with this man, or did you see him here that night or any night?"

"Billy is a regular here and he's a good customer. He doesn't get in fights and he loses more than he wins. We like people like that, so honestly, I didn't spend anytime wondering what him or any of his buddies were doing." Dereck held the phone in his hands. "He doesn't look familiar, but I can ask security to go through the footage that hasn't been deleted, looking for him."

"I'd appreciate that."

"Anything I can do to help." Dereck stood. "Henri was good man. I'm sorry about what happened."

"I wish I had known him." Troy shook Dereck's hand. "Thank you for your time." He made his way back across the room where Esme and everyone else in their group had been shown to a table.

Esme handed him a club soda with a lime. He eased into the booth and picked at some chips, contemplating his conversation with Dereck. Esme sat to his right, and next to her were Stone and Sparrow. To Troy's left were Clint and his wife Avery.

"Well?" Esme asked with an arched brow.

"Ashley used the right word when she said lurking." Troy leaned back and rested a possessive arm around Esme. Bile bubbled in his throat as he stared across the room at Billy.

Esme's ex-boyfriend.

Jealousy wasn't a good look on him and it didn't feel any better either.

He had no reason to be envious of their past relationship. They had dated when they were kids. Oh, hell. He'd almost gotten married when he'd been twenty. He thought his bride to be had been pregnant with child, only to learn that had been a bald-faced lie.

"He didn't recognize Brett, but that doesn't mean anything. He's a busy man when he's here," Troy said.

"I can't believe Brett is back in town." Sparrow lifted her soda and took a sip. "I haven't seen him in years and I can't say I want to either."

Troy didn't want to come off like a green-eyed boyfriend. He had a job to do and everyone at this table had been deemed *in the know.* But now he needed to find a way to do his job without coming off like an asshole. "There has been chatter at the fire station about Brett being in town, but it's like he's a ghost."

"Excuse me?" Esme jerked her head. "When did you find that out? And why didn't you tell me?"

The sound of slot machines ringing in the background grated on Troy's every nerve. "Trent told me right before we came here," he admitted. "I've been processing the intel, trying to put it in perspective."

"What exactly did your twin say?" Esme drew her lips into a tight line. "Are the rumors about the fire being brought up again? Because if they are, and you start poking that bear, you'll come to find out that both Sparrow and I were there that night and questioned as well. And not as witnesses. But as persons of interest."

"Along with thirty other teenagers. I was detained for eight hours just because of who my parents are." Sparrow laughed. "My father barged into the police station, making all sorts of threats. That part was actually kind of comical. I do tend to get off on watching my dad flex that muscle sometimes."

"That was a fun night." Esme lifted her drink and tapped it against Sparrow's. "Not. My dad was pissed and had half a mind to ask the sheriff to put me in a cell for shits and giggles. Billy too. I never understood that logic for something we didn't do, but I suspect he was angrier with the fact we'd all been drinking."

"I can't believe this is where the two of you just went." Troy reined in his frustration. This wasn't the time or place to allow his distress over feeling betrayed to get the better of him, especially when he didn't have the facts. "I don't understand why neither of you thought to tell me about this fire." He made sure his tone was level, but by the narrowed stare Esme gave him, he wasn't successful.

"It doesn't have anything to do with the issue at hand," Esme said. "Not to mention, you're not an investigator. I am. And Sparrow is handling this for the sheriff's department. And both Sparrow and I discussed it. Where's the connection? Because I'd have to look at every fire that claimed a life that Billy and Micky were at. I know of three off the top of my head. The motives don't match up."

"We're not going to start chest pounding now, are we?" Troy stiffened his spine. He didn't want to fight, but how the hell was he supposed to protect her if she didn't give him all the facts? It had nothing to do with motives or connecting the past to the present, though Troy's gut was as hot as a wild fire.

"Now, children, let's play nice in the sandbox," Clint said. "But I'm sitting here running all of this through my head and I'm not sure I understand how one is connected to the other. I can see the people connection, but not anything else."

"They aren't," Sparrow said. "Other than the fact that Billy and Micky had been at a party the night of the fire that killed three of our friends. But so had a lot of other kids." She held up her hand when Troy opened his mouth. "I understand that it feels like this is connected because Billy and Micky were in the fire that killed Henri, but the fires are different as well as the circumstances behind them. I'm willing to concede that Billy looks suspicious about something when it comes to the current fire. And if Henri was going to fire him and he knew it, that is a possible motive, but the Smith fire is something entirely different."

"All right. But I still want to know what

happened," Troy said. "All I know is that three girls died in that fire and someone by the name of Andrew Kimber went on trial for setting the fire but was acquitted. I don't think that's an unreasonable request."

"Hey," Clint interrupted. "Billy is heading to the poker room. I think I'll take my bride and keep an eye on him and look around for this Brett guy."

"Thanks, man," Troy said.

Clint tapped his knuckles on the table before taking his wife's hand and strolling across the casino floor.

Troy didn't like how the feelings of disloyalty filled his heart. Until he heard the story, he had no right to judge the reason it had been kept from him. It could be nothing.

But it could be everything.

He always told his brothers to listen to their gut; however, when it came to an investigation, unless they had facts to back it up, they could only use it as a compass.

Right now, his gut pointed to a smoking gun by the names of Billy and Brett. He wasn't sure about Micky since he was mortally wounded and they hadn't been able to interview him yet.

"I'm surprised you don't see how there could be a connection with the fire that was set sixteen years ago, and the fact your father was killed in a fire that hurt Micky and Billy was in the building." Troy understood that coincidences did happen, but this seemed too strange to be overlooked.

"If Brett had been in that building, or Andrew, my hackles would have been up, but my father worked with both Billy and Micky." Esme narrowed her stare. "Andrew had a motive to set the fire that killed Cathy Smith."

"And what was that?" Troy asked.

"Cathy pretended to like him. Got him to send dick pics and other embarrassing pictures of himself. She then made fun of him, posting the pictures on social media," Sparrow said. "I felt bad for the kid. I tried to be nice to him because I know what it's like to be ostracized. It's one of the reasons I dumped Brett. He could be a total asshole sometimes."

"What about Billy and Micky?" Troy asked. "Did he bully this young man too?"

"Not that I saw," Esme said. "But Billy didn't like Andrew and he's always believed Andrew started that fire."

"In his statement, Billy told the police that he'd overheard Andrew telling a friend at school that he was going to make Cathy pay for what she did," Sparrow said. "But I struggle to believe that."

"Micky and Brett both corroborated that story." Esme nodded. "However, the state couldn't produce any other witnesses to testify to that fact."

"The defense was also able to provide footage from a security camera in town showing Andrew walking down the street at the time the fire had started. It would have been impossible for him to get from the Smith's house and into town during that time frame without a car and he didn't have one," Sparrow said. "The state tried to find someone who might have picked him up or given him a ride, but nothing."

"In the end, the jury couldn't convict Andrew. As soon as the trial was over, his family moved and he's never been back." Esme lowered her head. "It changed my relationship with Billy. We stayed together on and off for another year and a half, but I realized that while he wasn't a horrible person, he was self-centered. Not someone I could be with."

"Is Brett still friends with Billy and Micky?" Troy took her hand and squeezed it. If anyone could understand caring for the wrong person, it was him and he wasn't going to shame her for that.

"Nope," Esme said. "If you think Billy has an ego, spend five minutes with Brett. It's bigger than the Grand Canyon. He's so full of himself it's disgusting."

"Not to mention he uses people and spits them out when he's done. Shortly after graduation, he was done with Billy and Micky and the rest of us. We weren't good enough for him and that was that." Sparrow folded her arms. "And I say good riddance."

"The one good change in Billy was that fire in some ways shaped his decision to become a firefighter," Esme said. "He told me that he'd never felt so helpless before. That waking up and finding out that some of our friends had died and there was nothing he could have done sealed his fate."

Troy let the information tumble around in his brain. He could understand why they didn't believe there was a connection. If he had lived through that, he might have come to the same conclusion. However, he was an outsider looking in and that always gave a person a different perspective.

And Billy and Micky were walking by that building for a reason.

They had parked farther way from the tavern for a reason.

Henri hadn't wandered inside for no reason.

"The one thing I haven't been able to find is your father's personal calendar," Troy said. "Ashley said he kept a separate one from the work one on his cell and on his computer."

Esme nodded. "It was a handwritten pocket one and he always carried it with him. I shouldn't assume anything, but I would guess he had it on him and it burned in the fire."

That made sense. "So, it's more than likely he was meeting someone there," Troy said.

"I've been thinking about that since he died." Esme sighed. "But I can't imagine…" Her eyes went wide and her lips parted. "You think he was meeting Brett?"

"I think he was following Brett here," Troy said.

"Why would he be meeting him?" Sparrow asked.

"And why would Brett still be in town if he had anything to do with the fire?" Stone leaned forward, resting his elbows on the table. "We're missing something and that's connected to who broke into Henri's house and clocked Esme on the head."

"I didn't have a good handle on what was in my dad's house, so I don't know what they could have been looking for." Esme pulled her hair over her shoulder and twisted the strands through her fingers. "Everyone in this town believes Andrew started the Smith fire. His job as a defense attorney is a bit of a joke."

"What is your take on the fire?" Troy asked.

"I read the file when I became an investigator," Esme said. "The entire downstairs was laced with accelerant. Three gas cans were found in the backyard. No prints. The three girls were trapped in Cathy's bedroom. They had no chance. Whoever started the fire locked them in, but there is no physical evidence to point the finger at anyone." Esme swiped at her eyes. "Even when you prove arson, it's hard to find who the culprit is because the fire destroys all the clues. Andrew is the only one who had motive," Esme said.

"That you know of," Stone added.

Esme nodded. "There is one other possibility that I know my father begged the police to look into and that was my mother and her followers."

Troy arched a brow. "Chuck Manzo has only been communicating with Heather for ten years. This fire happened sixteen years ago."

"That doesn't mean some other idiot who idolized her didn't come out of the woodwork and do it," Stone said.

"If that were the case, wouldn't we have seen a rash of fires? Or murders?" Troy asked. "What about that other man Chuck was writing to?"

"He didn't start fires. But I have to agree with that. It might not have happened in this area." Esme tapped her finger on the table. "My mom—Heather—started fires all across the state. I can cite serial firestarters who crossed state lines on their rampages. It all depends on what motivates them."

"If we go with Andrew starting the fire, it was pure revenge," Stone said. "That could be one and done."

"That's true," Sparrow said. "But an arsonist isn't going to be able to stop."

"I'll have my department pull up all unsolved arson fires in the state." Esme leaned back in her chair and sighed. "If it wasn't Andrew, which I never believed it was, even his motive was weak."

"I don't know about that," Stone said. "Bullying and revenge are huge motives. My mom has written many books on the subject."

"We all can agree he had reason to go after Cathy for what she did, but after the incident he always held his head high. He never backed down. At least not about being teased for the naked pictures," Esme said. "His social media posts became all about bullying and why we shouldn't give them power."

"So, he and his family moved away because everyone believed he murdered three girls," Troy said. "Why were Brett, Billy, and Micky questioned more so than other kids?"

"It wasn't just them. I was questioned pretty harshly too," Esme said.

"Why?" Troy asked.

"There was a rumor that Billy cheated on Esme with Cathy and that there might be photographic proof and Cathy was going to use it," Esme said. "But the reality was he dated Cathy before me and it's possible there was some overlap."

"That's sucky," Troy said.

"It was early on and it never happened again." She held up her hand. "I'm not making excuses for him, but I was young and stupid, and in some ways, I was using Billy."

"I'm agreeing with the stupid part," Sparrow said. "The other reason Jim homed in on the threesome was Sally Wilber thought she saw Brett's sports car leaving the house at one in the morning with two passengers."

"Sally Wilber? The reporter?" Stone asked.

"That's the one. But she was also dating Andrew at the time, so she was discredited," Esme said.

"When asked about it today, she'll tell you that she can't trust her memory of the night. She'd been drinking and while she knows she saw a car, she doesn't know whose car it was."

Troy stared at Esme. Her emotions rose to the surface, but they weren't solicited. She didn't have a good handle on what she was thinking or feeling, and Troy sensed that.

What confused him though was why he had such a tight connection to her when that was something reserved for his brothers.

"What's going on inside that pretty little head of yours?" Troy asked.

"We have all these dots that we can't connect. We don't even know if they are part of the equation. We all know that there are two things that will answer that for us. The first one is figuring out why my dad was in that building. The second one is finding out who broke into his house." She rubbed the back of her head. "I know I locked the door, but it was wide open when Sparrow and Stone got there and there was no sign of forced entry."

"Are you the only one with a key?" Troy asked.

"I thought so," Esme said. "But someone could have made one. Someone who visited him or someone from the office. It's not that hard if you know what you're doing."

Troy pinched the bridge of his nose. They needed

to simplify things. Break them down into bite-size pieces and put them back together slowly.

"Okay. We have three possible connections. Heather and her followers. Brett and the gang. Or an unknown threat that we haven't even thought of. But we have to find the motive as well. What is it that Henri had come across that got his hackles up? And that brings me right back to Billy."

"Because he was thinking about firing him?" Esme asked.

Troy nodded. "When was the last time your father changed the locks to his house?"

Esme stared at him and didn't say a single word. She didn't have to. Her silence conveyed the answer.

His cell buzzed.

"Well, well, well," he said. "Clint followed Billy into the parking garage and look at who he's meeting with." He held up his cell, showing a picture of Billy and Brett.

"Maybe Troy is onto something," Stone said, waving to the waitress with his credit card. "Why don't you two stay here and let Sparrow and me check this out."

"It might be fun to fake run into my ex with my husband." Sparrow jumped to her feet. She leaned over and kissed Esme on the cheek. "I'll call you later."

"Thanks." Esme sighed.

Troy stretched out his arm and shook Stone's hand. "Call if you need backup."

"Will do."

Troy watched with trepidation as Sparrow and Stone disappeared into the crowd. He knew he was making the right decision in letting them handle the situation. Both Stone and Clint were trained professionals and while they weren't his brothers, they were his brothers-in-arms.

That meant something.

"I know that wasn't easy for you to let them take over." Troy snagged his nonalcoholic drink, wishing he'd ordered the real thing.

"I bet you're breaking out in hives right about now."

"That's funny." He swirled the ice cubes around in his glass. He took a moment to organize his thoughts. "Has Billy ever talked about Brett over the years?"

"Not once and I can't say I've ever asked."

"How close are you and Billy?" Troy swallowed the green-eyed monster that reared its ugly head.

"We're not. Until my father died, I barely saw him. Or spoke to him."

"What was your breakup like?"

She tilted her head. "Are you asking as fire chief and someone who works for the Brotherhood Protectors or for a different reason?"

"Honestly? Both."

"That's fair," she said softly. "He wasn't happy

about it, which I found odd because the last few months all we did was fight over how I treated him."

"And how was that?"

She laughed. "No different than anyone else, but he thought I spoke down to him and he wanted me to be someone I wasn't. He didn't want to be equals. He asked me not to go to firefighting school. He begged me not to accept the job. It got worse when I outranked him at the station. He wants a little woman and I'm not that girl. When we broke up, we never worked the same shift, unless absolutely necessary. It wasn't ugly. It was silent. After I became a police officer, we didn't speak for almost three years until I pulled him over for speeding. That didn't go well. Worse when I wrote him a ticket and he accused me of getting off on my power."

"Did he ever do anything to hurt you or make you look bad in front of your peers?"

"I see where this is going," she said. "And the answer is complicated."

"It's a simple yes or no."

She shook her head. "He never tried to sabotage me or anything like that, but he did try to shake my confidence. Or question my authority. He will never like to take orders from a woman. Their place is in the home. So, there were times he said hurtful things, but he never did anything underhanded."

"I trust facts more than I trust my instincts, but right now, my gut is screaming that Billy at the very least knows something and he's not telling us," Troy said. "I'm going to call him into my office for a little chat tomorrow."

"I want to be there." Esme rested her hand on his shoulder.

"Not in the room, but we'll figure something out." He took her hand and laced his fingers through it. "I need you to trust me."

"Can you do the same with me?"

"Yes," he said. And he meant it.

CHAPTER 11

ESME LAY in Troy's bed and stared at the report from the fire that killed her father.

Arson.

There were four different points of origin when it came to where the fire had started. At least based on burn patterns.

Forensics also found traces of accelerants. Not much, but there had been enough that she could declare the fire wasn't an accident.

She let out a long breath.

Proving the fire had been set on purpose didn't give her any of the answers she needed. She still didn't know why her father had been in that house or why anyone wanted him dead. Her mind filled with a million more questions. Like why was Brett in town and having secret meetings with Billy? The last time she'd spoken to Billy about Brett, Billy acted as though he couldn't stand the man. Brett left Fool's Gold for greener pastures, and he had no intentions of ever looking back.

Could Troy be onto something when it came to connecting what happened at the Smith fire and the present situation?

It didn't make sense, and yet, it stuck in her brain like a migraine.

Troy had a unique way of looking at things, and she respected his opinion. She also had a deep emotional connection she couldn't explain. She'd never met anyone like him. Describing him as a gentleman only scratched the surface.

Most men she knew would have assumed they could join her for the night because they had slept together. But not Troy. He gave her a tender kiss goodnight by his office and told her if she needed anything at all, not to hesitate to wake him up.

He made no assumptions about being with her and waited for an invitation, which she opted not to give, and her body regretted that decision.

Her mind did as well.

Her heart, on the other hand, was torn. She had fallen for him hard and fast. Her dad had warned her about how love could sneak up on a person when they least expected it. He also told her to be careful of those first few flutters. He warned her that infatuation and true feelings could often be mistaken for one another and to give it time before expressing herself to the object of her affection.

Because of her father's wise words, jumping in with two feet was not something she'd ever done. As she got older, her dad often tried to tone down that advice, telling her that she took it too literally. That all he meant was that she needed to make sure that her gut, her head, her heart, and her soul all needed to match up.

And more importantly, take those first few weeks and months slowly. But that love at first sight did happen. It was real. She could trust her feelings.

But she needed to protect them.

She needed to make sure her emotions were on track with whoever she'd fallen in love with.

She wasn't in love with Troy. Was she? When she looked back on her life, she realized she hadn't ever been in love.

Billy had been her first real relationship. If she were being completely honest with herself, she dated him because he gave her something that not even her father could.

Acceptance with her peers.

Without Billy, she was the daughter of a serial arsonist and killer. It didn't matter that Heather hadn't raised her or that she didn't even remember her mother.

To a bunch of immature teenagers and their scared parents, biology made her a freak.

Billy gave her credibility.

She stayed with him out of fear of going back to being alone on an island. The only other person who understood had been Sparrow. However, Sparrow dealt with her problems differently. She used her parents' infamy to her advantage and it helped that her father wasn't in prison and was living his best life.

A tap at the door made her jump. "Yes," she managed.

"I hope I didn't wake you." Troy pushed open the barn-style door. He tucked a notebook under his arm. "I saw a light under the door, so I took a chance."

"Nope. I was studying the fire report." She waved her tablet. Maybe he wanted to slip in between the sheets after all. Her heart pounded heavily, rattling her rib cage. She told herself that if she invited him to her bed, that she would be using him. That it wouldn't mean anything.

He leaned against the doorjamb. "I need to step out for a moment. I won't be gone long."

"Where are you going?" Her pulse moved to her throat, making it hard to swallow.

"Just over to the bunkhouse where my brother Heath lives. I won't be more than a half hour or so.

But in case you came looking for me in my office, I didn't want you to worry."

"Is there something wrong?" She scooted into a sitting position, wrapping her arms around her knees.

Troy shook his head. "I just want to get another perspective on everything we've learned so far."

"Have you heard from Clint regarding Billy or Brett?"

"Clint followed Brett to an AirBnB a few blocks from the casino right after the meeting, which only lasted twenty minutes."

"So, nothing new." She rubbed her temples. "I want to go back to my father's house and search it."

"That's another thing I wanted to tell you," Troy said. "I just sent my brothers Trent and Marcus over there. They should be pulling out of the ranch now. I didn't want to wait."

"You should have discussed that with me first." She glared. This was the exact reason her father had warned her to take things slow. Women often showed their true colors much sooner than men. "I'm the investigator. Not you. That should be my call. Not to mention they are firefighters and not under my employment."

"I'm not trying to step on your toes or do things without you." He rubbed the back of his neck. "But this is also a Brotherhood Protectors case and my brothers are under their employ." He held up four fingers. "We know the fire was set on purpose. Someone may have a key to your dad's place. That means they might understand the security system, so they could have already been in and out." He lowered two fingers. "We were run off the road. It could have been a fluke, but neither one of us believe that." He waggled his index finger. "And this Brett guy is back in town, but it's like he doesn't want anyone to know. Waiting to search your father's house would be a mistake and having you do it a bigger one."

"I disagree with the last statement. I'm the best person." She tugged at her ponytail, releasing her hair. She ran her fingers through the strands. "I understand that Jake and Hank are concerned for my safety. I get that my boss, George, wants to protect the integrity of the investigation. I want all that too." She pushed down all the pain that threatened to bubble to the surface.

The horrifying sadness.

The loneliness that filled her heart knowing that she'd never be able to hug her father again.

Or hear his laugh.

See his smile.

Tell him how much she loved and appreciated him.

Henri Jade was gone.

And the only thing she felt she could do in his

memory was find answers and now this man whom she had all these swirling emotions for was blocking her from doing that.

"He was my father," she whispered, choking on the rawness of it all. "Now that we can prove arson, we need to prove murder."

Troy sat on the edge of the bed, setting his notebook aside, and took her hand. He ran his thumb tenderly over her skin.

She wanted to pull away. She wanted to reject his kindness.

His love.

But she couldn't.

"I want to find who started that fire." He kissed the back of her hand. "But I need to protect you too. So, please trust that I know what I'm doing."

She closed her eyes and counted to ten—backward—before blinking them open. "It's not easy for me to relinquish control to you and not just because it's my father who was killed."

"I know." Troy cupped her chin. "And understand that I'm not asking you to. I want you to be an active partner. But you need to let me take point. Can you do that?"

"I think so."

"Good." He tapped the notebook. "In here are a list of questions and topics to talk to Billy about. I was hoping you could go through them and make any adjustments or additions you think might be appropriate."

"Have you figured out how I'm going to be present, without being present?" she asked.

"I'll have a listening device in my office. You'll be able to hear the entire conversation."

"Thank you."

He leaned in and kissed her cheek. "If the light is on, I'll let you know I've returned."

The last thing she wanted to do was sound desperate. She cleared her throat and tucked her hair behind her ears. "Don't look for a sign. Just join me."

OF ALL HIS BROTHERS, Heath was honestly the last person, outside of Marcus, he would have picked to go to for advice about women. Not because he didn't value Heath, he did, but of all the Falco boys, Heath was more of a loner. The older Heath got, the better he'd become at being engaged in group activities.

But only because Troy pushed.

Troy rounded the corner to the main door of the bunkhouse and laughed. "What the hell are you doing?" He stared at Heath, who sat in front of a small fire next to a tent.

"What does it look like?"

Troy handed Heath a soda and pulled up an

Adirondack chair. He twisted off the cap to his beer. "Are you sleeping out here?"

"It's a nice night, and I've got a flap in the tent to look at the stars." Heath cracked open his beverage. "I figure while it's still warm out, I might as well enjoy the weather."

"I guess that makes sense."

"Now, what the hell are you doing when you've got a good-looking woman keeping your bed warm?" Heath arched a brow. "Or am I not reading that situation right and my brotherly intuition is off since I'm not your twin."

"No. You're spot-on, but I'm sure Trent already told you."

"Yeah. There are no secrets in this family." Heath leaned forward, snagging another log, and tossed it on the fire. "What's the problem?"

"When you left home, I was sixteen."

"I remember."

"I had just started dating Darlene."

Heath rolled his eyes. "She was not good enough for you, man."

Troy laughed. "You made that clear when you told me she was going to break my heart someday. The next morning, you were gone."

"I couldn't live with Dad anymore. Besides, I had my own demons to deal with."

Heath spent a few years battling drug and alcohol addiction. He was clean and sober now, but there was a time where Troy truly worried about his brother and what might happen to him if he continued down that path.

"I know, but at the time, I thought you were being an asshole and I didn't listen," Troy said. "You had nothing to back up your statement."

Heath tapped the center of his chest. "My Falco instincts told me she wasn't going to do right by you, but you rejected that philosophy. You needed cold, hard facts. I didn't have that."

"I thought she loved me for nearly four years. She took away my ability to understand women, much less trust how they feel about me."

"Bullshit," Heath said. "That's a cop-out and you know it."

"Are you kidding me?" Troy had replayed what happened between him and Darlene a million times and he could never make any sense of it. The one time he talked to her after she left him standing at the church, looking like a fool, she'd given him a nonanswer. "What kind of person fakes a pregnancy to get a man to marry them and then doesn't show up?"

"The kind of woman who realized she wasn't going to be able to pull it off for the long haul." Heath set his drink on the ground and leaned forward. "What did Darlene tell you about why she didn't show up to the wedding?"

Troy took a hearty swig. He remembered the words exactly. He tilted his head toward the sky and stared at the stars. "She said, *I can't live like this anymore. There is no baby. There never was and I can't marry you. I shouldn't have forced your hand. I don't love you. I only loved the idea of you.* Then she hung up. I tried calling her back for days, but she never answered. Her parents wouldn't speak to me or tell me anything. When I returned home to take care of Dad, I learned she got married two years after she dumped me and has three kids. She lives in Utah somewhere." He ran a hand across the top of his head and shifted his gaze back to his brother. "If she didn't love me, why did she fake a pregnancy to get me to marry her?"

"Did she know the guy she married while she was still with you?"

"He graduated from high school the year before Seth, but I believe she at least knew who he was," Troy admitted.

"Could she have been cheating on you?" Heath asked. "There was a lot going on in your life back then between all the bullshit Dad was putting you through, not to mention the crap I was doing and Trent leaving for the Air Force."

"We did fight a lot about how disconnected I was and she had been super annoyed with me when it came to how much attention I paid to Marcus. Our relationship was in turmoil and she thought the only way to fix it was for me to get out of Dad's house and for us to be married. I wasn't on board with that at all. Not until she told me she was pregnant. That changed everything."

"Falcos always live up to their responsibilities," Heath said, quoting their father. "I'm sure Darlene had heard him say that a time or two."

"She'd heard me say it all the time." Troy let out a short laugh. "You're smarter than you look." Troy hadn't wanted to believe that Darlene had cheated on him. Whenever he went down that rabbit hole, he always came back to how she trapped him into marriage and how those things didn't fit together.

Only, they did in this case.

"You didn't come out here to talk about Darlene," Heath said. "So, what is it about Esme that has you questioning whether or not she has any real feelings for you?"

"Because it's all happening fast, hard, and intense. And it's mixed in with this investigation with her dad."

"I can see how that would cloud things." Heath leaned back. "You have always been the most level-headed of the five of us brothers. You use your instincts as a compass, guiding you, but you don't let them rule you because you believe in facts."

"I came here because I wanted you to tell me something I don't know."

"I'm getting to that." Heath laughed. "The way you do things at work is amazing. You're a natural-born leader. Probably better than any of us. You have style and grace when it comes to directing people. Your concept of instinct versus facts is perfection in the workplace. But, dude, it sucks when it comes to people and that includes women and your love life." He pressed his hand in the center of his chest. "I might not be marriage or long-term relationship material, but the one thing I do know is that I always follow my gut feelings when it comes to people. What does your gut and your heart tell you about Esme?"

"That she's the real deal, but I—"

"Don't you dare tell me that you felt that way about Darlene, because I still have the letters you wrote me and you flat-out told me that you had a bad feeling about the relationship before it ended."

Troy snapped his mouth shut. Heath was right. For months before Darlene told him she was with child, he'd contemplated breaking up with her because the stress of his home life and dealing with the pressures of her wanting to be married and have kids of her own was too much.

"Stop using her as your excuse to push people away," Heath said. "If you care about Esme and want to be with her, go for it."

Troy jumped to his feet. "Thanks, man."

"Anytime," Heath said. "Just remember who set you straight when it comes time to ask for a best man."

TROY SHED his clothing and slipped between the sheets as quietly as possible. She had invited him into her bed, but he wasn't going to wake her. Not tonight. All he wanted or needed was to wrap his arms around her and hold her through the night.

"Troy?" She shifted. "What time is it?"

"Shhhh," he whispered. "Go back to sleep."

Her hand found his hip, and her nails tickled his skin.

He closed his eyes, determined to ignore the pull to ravish her body, but she continued to torture him with gentle strokes. "You're making it impossible for me to be a gentleman and let you get your beauty rest."

"Are you serious? You climbed in naked."

"I always sleep that way," he said. "And you don't have anything on either." He cupped her breast, pinching and twisting her hard nipple. The game was over. There was no turning back now. But he didn't want to. His heart and soul were connected to hers in ways he couldn't explain.

"Oh, don't stop doing that."

He wrapped both arms around her glorious body. He kissed her neck, tasting her sweetness. He adored everything about her and wanted to show her how much. He'd do anything for her.

She rolled over, curling her fingers around his length.

He groaned as she kissed the center of his chest and made her way down his stomach. "What are you doing?"

"Giving you pleasure." She glanced up, smiling.

"That's my job."

"Not this time." She pushed him to his back and brought him to her sweet lips.

He swallowed. Hard.

Pooling her hair on top of her head, he watched as he disappeared into her mouth. He gasped for air. His lungs burned as he tried to fill them with oxygen.

He tugged her off him a little too harshly and pulled her from the mattress, bending her over the bed. Grabbing the condom from the nightstand, he quickly wrapped himself in one and slammed himself inside her with a deep thrust.

"Yes," she said. "Please. I need you."

He was desperate to fill her. He wrapped his arm around her, finding her hard nub. Holding himself inside, he fanned his fingers across her in a circular motion.

Her hips rolled up and down, grinding against him in an exotic dance while her climax spilled onto him like hot lava. She cried out his name, arching her back.

His orgasm came seconds after hers in an intense, mind-crushing moment. It took his breath away.

Moments later he collapsed on the bed, holding her as tight as he could, their bodies still shaking. He kissed her shoulder. "I care about you, Esme." He wanted to say so much more, but he didn't want to scare her away.

She dropped her arm and leg over him and sighed. "You're unexpected and I like you too."

CHAPTER 12

Esme jerked awake. "What was that?" She blinked. The sky had begun to lighten with the morning, but it was still dark outside. She had no idea what had startled her, but she knew it wasn't the man whose arms had been protecting her all night.

"I'm not sure, but it sounded like breaking glass." Troy jumped to his feet. He found his jeans, hiked them up over his hips, and snagged his weapon from the dresser. "Stay here."

"Like hell." She stumbled from the bed in search of something to put on her naked body before grabbing her gun. "You forget, I was a police officer for five years."

He chuckled. "Nope. I'm just one of those idiot men who sometimes forgets they are with a woman who is probably more capable than they are."

"That's the nicest thing you've ever said to me."

She peered over his shoulder as he crept out into the corridor. "Do you smell that?" She stuck her nose in the air and inhaled deeply.

"Smoke," he said. "And I can taste gas too."

"Are your brothers still on the ranch?"

"Yes," he whispered. "But their shift starts at seven, so they are awake, and I texted Seth. He and the rest of my brothers are on their way."

The stable had two access points. The main door to the left and a smaller one to the right. "Shall we split up?"

"Yes," he said. "Don't open that door if you think someone is out there or if—"

"Don't worry about me," she said before heading to the right. She kept her weapon raised, inching into each stall, her senses in hyperdrive. The closer she got to the far end, the less she could smell the smoke.

"Esme, come here," Troy shouted. He waved his hand from the doorway of his office.

She bolted down the center of the stables. "What is it?" Her heart thumped in the center of her chest. She skidded to a stop at the opening of Troy's office, where he was hunched over his desk, tapping on the keyboard. "What's happening?"

"Someone breached the ranch and started a fire." He pointed to the third monitor. "Both doors are barricaded."

"So, we're trapped." She rested her hand on her neck. Her throat tightened. She coughed.

Troy glanced over his shoulder. "We're fine. The fire hadn't been going on too long. Seth and Trent are putting it out now as we speak." He pointed to the screen, which showed his brothers holding hoses, dousing the fire. "When it's safe, they will open the doors. Heath is doing a perimeter check on foot and Marcus is firing up his helicopter. He's going to check things out from the air. My cameras, the ones I have set up, record, so we'll be able to see who did this."

"Have they called it in? Because I don't think they should," Esme said.

Troy tilted his head. "Why not?"

"Our list of suspects is short and weak. But we can see people's reactions when they see we are not only unharmed and unfazed, but that it was a nonevent, instead of something potentially horrific."

He curled his fingers around her neck and kissed her hard. "I like the way you think."

"And here I thought you'd tell me it didn't follow protocol."

"Yeah, well, I can bend the rules." He winked. "Sometimes."

She laughed. "Once in a blue moon, I bet."

"Oh, the moon was pretty last night." He pulled out his chair and sat down. "Whoever was here was smart, but not brilliant."

"Why do you say that?" She rested her hands on his shoulders and shifted her gaze between three screens. One screen was lit up like a Christmas tree. A dark figure came into view. The person was tall and thick. Most likely a man based on body type, but not necessarily. He wore a black ski mask as well as a dark sweater and jeans. He tossed a rock at the light, making it difficult for her to see him anymore.

"That's why." Troy tapped the screen. "Whoever that person is, he has blue eyes."

"Both Billy and Brett have blue eyes," Esme said. "But so does Chuck Manzo."

"Yeah, but Chuck had black hair. That man has brown hair. And straight. Like Billy or Brett."

"That's still inconclusive." Esme set her gun on the table. "There are a lot of people in Fool's Gold who fit that description."

"True." Troy turned, taking her by the hips and bringing her to his lap. "But that man didn't wear gloves, possibly leaving fingerprints behind. I've already texted my brothers to get someone out here to dust. If it's Billy, we have his prints in the system."

"We have Brett's too."

"We do?" Troy asked.

"They took them the night of the Smith fire." She wrapped her arms around her shoulders. "I'm forming some thoughts that I don't like and it makes me concerned for Micky."

"I'm listening."

"What if my father learned something new about

the Smith fire and went to the condemned building not just to meet someone, but to confront them."

"That's exactly what I was thinking," Troy said.

"Micky can't talk. What if he was going to and—"

"I've already gotten the Brotherhood Protectors to put a man on his door twenty-four seven," Troy said. "Even if he wasn't going to spill the beans and he was collateral damage, when he wakes up, he's our only witness." He sighed. "Only, he's not doing well. He's still listed in critical condition."

"There are some other things I've been thinking about," she said. "When Brett left town, he did so on shaky ground with his parents. He and his father have always had a difficult relationship."

"Why is that?"

"Brett expected his father to hand him over the keys to the family business. He thought, because he came from money, that he should be given whatever he wanted. He hated that his father made him work. He stole money from his dad. He took the car when he wasn't supposed to, and his dad even once called the cops on him. For the most part, it all seemed like typical teenage rebellious stuff, but there are rumors out there that Brett has made his fortune through illegal means."

"Yes. But nothing has ever been proven," Troy said. "I skimmed through the Smith fire reports before I came to bed. There wasn't enough evidence to arrest Brett, but he was as strong of a suspect as

Andrew was based on Sally Wilber's account of the evening."

"She waffled in her statement as time passed."

"How do Billy and Sally feel about each other?" Troy asked.

"He didn't even really know who she was until our senior year. Sally flew under the radar. She was a bit of a bookworm. Spent more time in the library than hanging out with friends. She had always been on the school newspaper, but our senior year, she really came out of her shell when she started working for the local news station. She was totally into investigative journalism and when the dick pictures were sent out and the bullying of Andrew started, she was all over that. She was the one who uncovered that it was Cathy Smith who sent them. That's when Sally and Andrew became an item."

Troy's forehead wrinkled. "How long did Cathy and Andrew date?"

"Not long. They broke up right after the Smith fire."

"Was it because of the pictures?"

"I don't think so," Esme said. "After it had been proven that Cathy posted them and appropriate action had been taken, like being suspended from school and other measures, Andrew wanted to leave it alone. He wanted to move on with his life. But Cathy wanted to do a series of exposé articles about his experience. He told her that one television interview was enough. Cathy and her friends had all paid a price and everyone in school would think twice before they bullied anyone. I know they had a few heated discussions about it, but Sally couldn't let it go. She did a series on what happened, and Andrew wasn't happy. I know he thought it made it worse for him, and then the fire happened."

"You mentioned that Sally is the only reporter worth talking to, yet you don't feel all warm and fuzzy with her now," he said.

"She's a great reporter. Completely fair. She never tilts a story one way or the other, which is why I'm always happy to be interviewed by her, but sometimes it's to a fault. She doesn't have the same passion she used to and she's completely given up investigative reporting. It's as if she's afraid to hurt people."

"Do you think what Sally did hurt Andrew? I mean, bullying is a real problem."

"I can have someone pull the old news reels for you and you can decide for yourself, but in my humble opinion, I believe she made it personal, saying things about Cathy and her friends that in turn could be considered revenge bullying," Esme said. "It feels awfully weird to be sitting here having this discussion while there is a fire outside." She focused on the monitor that ran in real time. Seth and Trent were still holding hoses, dousing the stables with water, though it appeared the fire had been stamped out. She couldn't see any sparks or red flashes, but it was better to be safe than sorry.

Troy cupped her face. "We both know we're safe." He pressed his lips against her mouth.

She caved to his tender kiss. His tongue found hers and twisted and twirled in a familiar dance. Her body tingled with desire. Her heart swelled with passion. Her soul filled with kinship.

Troy was everything she'd ever wanted in a man, and more. Her father would have loved him and she wished desperately that they could have met. She could feel her dad smiling down as if to approve.

"You two can stop playing suck face now," a deep voice snapped her into the present.

She buried her face in Troy's neck. Heat rose to her cheeks.

"Very funny," Troy said. He lifted her from his lap and stood. "What's the damage?" He kept a strong arm around her waist. His hand squeezed her hip, but he was all business and she appreciated that about him, even though the embarrassment of being caught like a couple of teenagers lingered in her system.

"It's minimal," Seth said. "We found this." He held up a pentagram sign with a note which read: *cleansing this evil place of demons as the good Lord has commanded.*

"What do you make of it?" Trent asked. "Could that be one of your mom's followers?"

"It appears that way," Esme admitted. "My mom

did leave pentagrams, but her notes were different. They were more rants and long-winded. Specific to the fire and what demons she thought she was banishing. It was almost a homemade spell mixed with scripture, but that was also never given to the press, so people wouldn't know unless my mom told them."

"So, this could be someone pretending to be one of your mom's wannabes," Seth said.

"It could be. What else can you tell us about the fire and how it behaved?" She put on her investigative hat.

"The smell of gas is prevalent." Trent stood in the doorway. "I bet if I tested the building, the perimeter was doused in accelerant. The fire, however, flamed out fast. At first glance, whoever did this, wanted this place to go up like a motherfucker and they wanted the two of you to perish in the flames, only the pattern is a bit odd."

Esme shivered.

"Did you really need to be that graphic?" Troy asked. "I think we understood the intention when we were woken up and smelled smoke."

"It's okay." Esme took Troy's hand and laced her fingers through his. She had always considered herself a strong person, and this situation was no different. Granted, her life, for the third time since her father had died, had been challenged, but as a fire and arson investigator, as well as a former police officer and firefighter, this wasn't the first time her life had been in danger. "What else can you tell us about what went on outside?"

"Not much, ma'am." Seth raked a hand across the top of his head. A trait she noticed all the men in the Falco clan did, especially when they were either contemplative or potentially avoiding a discussion.

In this case, she believed Seth was contemplative.

"I've looked at the footage that Troy's security cameras captured," Seth said. "And Heath is still doing recon, but we don't believe there were more than two people on the premises."

"We only saw the one person on the cameras," she said.

"There are tire tracks at the main gate with two sets of footprints in the dirt," Trent said. "Making me a little happy we haven't paved the driveway yet."

"Heath's doing his own brand of forensics out there since we're not calling in the cavalry," Seth said. "But the Brotherhood Protectors will help us with that, no problem."

"Yeah, but what is there really to go on?" Troy asked. "I mean, do we have good footprint molds? And what about the integrity of the fire itself? Any chance of fingerprints?"

"I'm hopeful on the fingerprints, especially on the barricades," Seth said. "But they will only give us guidance if they are in the system. I don't think the molds will help us, but we're going to take them anyway."

"Are you sure you don't want us to call in the team?" Trent asked. "And I don't mean the fire station or even the local police. But we have so many other resources at our fingertips."

"Outside of the Brotherhood Protectors, no," Troy said.

Esme didn't like flying solo. However, bringing in anyone outside of the tight-knit group they had formed for this mission could be disastrous.

There were too many unknowns.

"We need to at least fill in Sparrow." Esme held Troy's stare.

"Agreed." Troy gave her a quick nod.

"We can't be late to the station," Trent said. "We'll make sure everything gets to the proper channels."

"All you need is new locks and you can still stay here," Seth said. "Cameras are still up and running. We'll all be safe."

"I have no doubt about that," Troy said.

"What about my father's house?" She shifted attention to Trent. "You and Marcus searched it last night. Did you find anything?"

"As a matter of fact, we did." Trent reached in his back pocket and pulled out a plastic bag with a folded piece of paper. "This was taped underneath the laundry basket in the guest room."

"That's an interesting place to hide something."

Esme took the plastic baggie and held it up in the air between two fingers as if it were something delicate that could break. She studied it, terrified to open it. "What made you look there?"

"No stone unturned," Troy said. "It's a motto we've always lived by."

Her pulse thumped in the center of her chest, beating its way across her body. "What is it?"

"Billy's official walking papers," Seth said. "Signed and sealed."

"Marcus and I had literally just pulled in when you called about the break-in." Trent stuffed his hands in his pockets. "On our way in, we passed two vehicles. I don't remember plates, because there was no reason to check them, but I do remember their make, model, and year. I'll get Sparrow to give me a rundown on possible owners."

"What were they?" Esme asked. A lot of folks in Fool's Gold all owned similar vehicles, but there were a few that stood out.

"A jacked-up Bronco, new and the other was a BMW SUV, also new," Trent said. "Both nice-looking rides."

"The vehicle that ran us off the road was a sporty BMW SUV." Esme swallowed. Hard. "And Billy bought a Bronco about two months ago. He loves that stupid thing. Drives it around like it's a prize bull." She took in a deep breath, holding for a count of ten before letting it out with a big swish. "My father fired him," she whispered. "His review had already happened and my dad canned him." She glanced at the paperwork. "Why wasn't this filed?" Her mind ran in a million directions but landed on one thing. "Could my dad have been negotiating Billy's employment for intel on something like who started the fire at the Smith's house?"

"That's exactly what I was thinking." Troy rested his hands on her shoulders.

She turned. "If that's the case, and Brett killed my father and tried to kill Micky, Billy could be in danger."

"Billy could also be part of the problem," Troy whispered. "I know you don't want to believe that, but we need to be open to both paths."

She stepped out into the corridor of the stable and glanced in both directions. Billy could be a bully. He could be arrogant. And he could be mean.

But a killer?

"We only see one person on the security camera. Why do you think that is?" Esme wasn't really looking for anyone to answer. Her mind needed to sort through the checklist that had formed. Performing her job to the best of her ability was priority. "Possibility number one is that suspect number two knew where the security cameras were and only wanted his partner to be caught on camera."

"That's an interesting theory," Seth said.

"Another option is he went searching for something else." Esme folded her arms and paced in the hallway. The action helped her think.

"I don't have the entire system set up, so we do have some weak spots, but all the main access points are covered." Troy sat in front of his computer once again and tapped away at the keyboard. "I've scanned the security cameras for all the buildings. The interlopers didn't go anywhere near them. But I can see two shadows race through the trees here." Troy tapped a key and pointed to one of the screens where he paused the video. "And again here; however, suspect number two stops right here and doesn't move." Troy pointed to the middle screen. "It appears he watched the other one do all the dirty work."

"Why?" Trent asked. "They could have gotten in and out faster if they had worked together."

"Culpability," Esme said. "The one who watched didn't actually do anything. He's not guilty, except for he watched and we have that on video."

"Wait a second." Troy shifted in his chair and pounded the keys. The computer hummed and the images flew across the screen. "Our intruder took out the light. Not the camera. He should have taken out both, making him kind of stupid. What if he did that on purpose? I mean, he looked the camera in the eye." Troy froze the screen.

Esme took leaned over Troy's shoulder. It had been a long time since she gazed into Billy's eyes and she couldn't be positive. "That's Billy. Or at least I believe those baby blues belong to him."

"That won't stand up in a court of law," Troy said. "But let's run with that for a little bit. Why would he allow himself to be captured like that on film? And then start a fire?"

"I need to see the fire pattern." Esme sucked in a deep breath and stood tall.

"Follow me," Seth said.

She raced back to Troy's bedroom and slipped on a pair of shoes and found her ponytail holder before heading toward the main door. The stable still smelled like smoke, but now her nose picked up the lingering scent of gasoline. She stepped outside and took ten steps back, staring at the door as Seth shut it.

Trent pointed to an object on the ground. It looked like a rake or some kind of garden tool. "That was used to keep the door locked from the outside."

She stepped over the burnt ground and touched the building, which had been slightly damaged, looked discolored, was a little warm to the touch, but otherwise fine. She pressed her nose about five feet from the ground and then inched lower and lower.

Gas became more prevalent, but it was the grass and dirt that smelled the worst.

Not the building itself.

"I want to watch the footage of Billy spraying the building," she said.

"That footage is limited to the doorways. And he did get those good. Thoroughly soaked them," Troy said as if to read her mind.

"Okay, but look at the fire pattern. Trent was right. It's weird." She wiggled her finger at the door and then at the ground. "It's not hugging the structure. It's going where the accelerant was placed." She strolled twenty paces to her right. "Every so often he splashed a little on the building, but not much." He pressed her hand on the side of the stable where a burn pattern inched up the building. "When you get over here, he doesn't hit the building at all. It goes a good ten feet from it."

"It's very possible that you could have escaped this fire thanks to the person who set it," Trent said.

"This changes how I approach Billy today and the questions I want to ask him." Troy raked a hand across his head. "We need the autopsy report on your dad."

"I was promised that today," Esme said. "Why don't we stop at the medical examiner's office on the way to yours and put some pressure on."

"Good idea," Troy said. "It would be nice to have those details before spending some alone time with Billy."

The sound of a helicopter overhead caught her attention. She glanced up. It came in low and hot as it headed for the hangar on the property.

Marcus.

"We need to get to the fire station," Seth said. "Stay in touch and if we hear any chatter, we'll let you know."

"Thanks, man." Troy slapped his brother on the back.

She stood there and stared at the stable. Tears stung her eyes. "Why would Billy do this? It doesn't make sense. I get he's an arrogant ass, but—"

"Hey." Troy cupped her face and brushed his mouth over hers in a loving kiss. "Don't do this to yourself. Don't go down that rabbit hole."

"Part of me has to," she managed with a shaky voice. "It's my job to ask all these questions."

"You're making it personal."

"He was my father and Billy at one point was my boyfriend." She pressed her hand over Troy's lips. "Of course it's personal. But don't you see the disconnect? He survived the fire that killed my father and nearly killed one of his best friends. We don't know why my dad was there. A question that has to be answered. But now Billy is starting fires while someone else watches, but that fire isn't what it seems to be or maybe even what the person watching wants."

"What are you suggesting?" Troy asked.

"Someone has something on Billy and they are using it to control his actions right now. But what he did with this fire is a cry for help."

CHAPTER 13

Esme flipped through the medical examiner's report. "Hey, George," she said as she tapped her cell phone, putting it on speaker. "I'm looking at the findings now."

Murdered.

Bullet to the head.

Point-blank range.

"I'm so sorry," George said. "Do you want me to send Colby? He's up to speed and can take over."

"No. I need to follow this through. Besides, I have a lot of help with Team Falco."

"I'm hearing rumblings that Fool's Gold is talking about making Troy the permanent fire chief."

"That would be an excellent choice. He's not only a fine leader, but he has skills in all areas. I'm impressed, and we know that's hard to do."

"It sure is," George said. "Do you want to talk through the ME report or anything else?"

Esme rubbed her temples. Her mind tumbled into the investigation. "How could anyone be so stupid as to not realize we would find out that my dad had been shot when we found his remains?"

Billy.

Micky.

They were at the scene. What the hell did they have to do with it? Could they have killed her father and were trying to cover it up?

And why?

Then there was Brett. What role did he have in all this? Because it couldn't be a coincidence that he was sneaking around town as if he hadn't returned.

"There are people who think a fire will cover up everything. As if it's hot enough to cremate a body," George said.

That statement made her think that there was no way it could have been Micky or Billy. They knew better.

But not Brett.

There was always the possibility that Billy's statement was true. That he and Micky were walking by the building, saw a fire, and leaped into action.

Even as she ran that scenario across her brain, something still didn't settle right.

And that was Billy's walking papers. Why had her

father fired Billy but not filed the paperwork? There had to be a reason.

"Something doesn't add up," she said. "I don't believe Billy's account of what went down."

"Is it all gut, or do you have something more substantial to back it up?"

"I've got something, but I'm not prepared to tell you yet."

"All right. I trust you," George said. "Keep me posted."

"Thanks." She ended the call and leaned back in her father's—no, Troy's—big leather chair and swiveled left and right. She tilted her head toward the ceiling and blinked her eyes closed, willing her father's memory to fill her mind.

Talk to me, Daddy.

Whenever she'd been stuck during an investigation, her father would always sit down with her and walk her through the important parts, separating out what she needed to focus on and what was frivolous.

In this case, what would her father have her connect?

Was the Smith fire important?

Yes.

Could her mother and her followers have anything to do with this?

That seemed unlikely at this point, but she had to consider the pentagon stars left at the fires.

Troy's pine scent filled her nostrils. She peeked open her eyes as he strolled into his office. "How are you holding up?"

"I'm the same as the last time you asked me that question," she mused.

"That's better than the alternative." He sat on the edge of the desk, holding a file in his hands. "I've pushed Billy to after lunch."

"Why? I'm ready for him."

"So am I, but we'll be even more ready after we speak to Andrew Kimber." Troy glanced at his watch. "He'll be here in fifteen minutes."

"Andrew agreed to meet in Fool's Gold, with you, to discuss the Smith fire?"

Troy's left eye twitched. "He contacted me."

She bolted upright. "Are you serious?"

Troy nodded. "I just got off the phone."

"What did he say, exactly?" Esme pressed her hands on the big wooden desk and stood. The weight of her job filled her system. It wasn't just that this was her father who had been murdered, but a potential fire that had killed three of her friends and was still unsolved hung in the balance. "And why didn't he call me? I'm the investigator. You're just the fire chief."

"Ouch. That hurt." He patted his chest. "But to your latter question, he thought it might be too hard for you." Troy held up his hand. "I quickly corrected him and informed him that you'd be at the meeting."

"Thank you."

Troy gave her a short smile. "As to the former question, he told me that your father had contacted him a few weeks ago."

"Why is he just now reaching out?"

"This is where it gets weird," Troy said. "There was a fire at his house the day before your father died. He suffered some smoke inhalation and burns, as did his wife. His children were treated for the same, but no one was hurt badly. He hadn't heard of the news until last night."

"Oh, my God. Do we know if his fire was accidental?"

"Not yet, but I had Ashley call over to your boss, asking to have Colby look into it," Troy said.

"That's one too many fires involving the same players to be a coincidence."

TROY DIDN'T KNOW what to expect during any of the upcoming interviews, but he knew he needed to protect Esme.

To anyone else, she was a well put together woman who could handle anything, and she could. Everywhere he went, people told him what a rock star she was and how she, of all people, could weather any storm.

But Troy could feel her emotions swirling around

his office like a twister. She may not wear them on her sleeve; however, he soaked them up like a sponge. He was drowning in her sadness and frustration. He didn't mind; only, he wished he could take away all the pain so she didn't have to feel any of it.

A tap at the door made him jump.

He glanced up to see Ashley standing there with a tall, skinny man who wore dark glasses and had dark thinning hair.

"Troy, this is Andrew Kimber."

"It's nice to meet you." Troy stood, waving Andrew into his office.

Esme stepped from the corner where she'd been pacing in a circle. "Hi, Andrew," she said softly. "It's been a long time."

"Esme. I'm so sorry to hear about your father." Andrew raised his arms, showing off a bandage on his left hand. He gave Esme a short embrace, kissing her cheek.

"We just heard about the fire at your home. That must have been terrifying," Esme said.

Andrew nodded his head once, blinking. "When the detectors went off, I immediately thought of the Smith fire. My wife and I sprang into action, making sure our children were safe, but Esme, I smelled gasoline. I know that fire wasn't an accident."

"We've asked for a special investigation," Esme said.

"I learned that on the way over. Thank you."

Andrew made himself comfortable in one of the chairs in front of Troy's desk.

Esme sat in the other one.

Troy rolled up the big leather chair and pulled out his notebook and pen. "When you called me, you mentioned you'd been talking with Henri. Can you tell me what that was all about?"

"Sure," Andrew said. "He called me asking about the Smith fire, which is something I don't generally discuss anymore. I went on trial for something I didn't do. People pointed their fingers at me because a girl bullied me, so they thought I wanted revenge. That wasn't true. I did want her to pay for what she did and the school suspended her, but she felt no pain. That was my only regret. Especially since she and her friends did this kind of thing to lots of guys; only, they caved to their demands."

"What are you talking about?" Esme leaned forward.

"The sex tapes and naked pictures that sometimes circulated around school." Andrew took off his glasses and stared at Esme with a puzzled expression. "I know you know about Robbie Dalton and Dino Myers. They were humiliated by what Leslie and Tabitha did."

"Leslie and Tabitha?" Troy jotted down their names. "As in the girls who perished in the fire with Cathy Smith?"

"Hang on. They were just as embarrassed. They

insisted they didn't know the pictures and videos had been taken. They accused Robbie and Dino of secretly taping them and sharing it with others, setting off a chain of events until everyone in the school had it." Esme pulled her hair over her shoulder and twisted it between her fingers.

Troy had noticed she did this when her brain rolled information around and rearranged it, trying to make sense of it.

"During my trial, my attorney and his private investigator spent a fair amount of time on the angle that Cathy and her friends were extorting fellow classmates with damaging pictures and videos. If they didn't pay or do whatever they wanted, they would release the tapes, like they did with Robbie and Dino. This was in my statement. It was supposed to be part of my defense, but the judge decided there wasn't enough evidence and both Robbie and Dino denied ever being threatened. We tried to find evidence that the girls had done this to others, but no one would talk."

"I had heard rumors that a couple of our class-mates might have been blackmailed." Esme dropped her hands to her lap. "I followed the trial. I read all the reports, including what Sally did for the school paper and that angle wasn't pushed."

"My lawyers didn't think it would be a good look since we had no hard facts to back it up," Andrew said.

"What did Cathy expect you to do in exchange for keeping the photos from going public?" Troy asked. "Money?"

"No. Favors. In my case, she wanted me to write papers for her and do other school-related things. It was stupid and I could have easily done it, but when I walked down the hallway after we'd hooked up and she ridiculed me, I knew there would be no way I'd put up with her and her bullshit. I understood then she was a power-hungry girl and I wasn't going to be her pawn. Or anyone's for that matter. That's when I made the decision to let her go public with the pictures and stand up to her."

"That was courageous," Troy said.

"She kept coming after me. She was relentless," Andrew said. "She told me she'd make up lies if I didn't do what she wanted. But there was no way in hell I would cower to her or her friends. I thought if I held my head up high, things would die down, and then Sally wrote her series and things got worse."

"Did Sally discuss her articles with you?" Troy had skimmed them and thought they were well done, especially since Sally had only been a teenager when she wrote them. However, they were slanted in the favor of Andrew and didn't paint a very nice picture of Cathy or her friends. Troy didn't have enough information regarding the situation to know if Sally had the facts correct. And there were some pieces that he figured were personal accounts and never proven. That was a problem in pieces like that.

But the two people sitting in his office should know enough.

"Yes and no," Andrew said. "She had expressed interest in doing an exposé on bullying, using my situation as the backdrop. I told her to please find a different angle. And then she dropped the bomb about how she knew about other kids who had done embarrassing things for Cathy and her friends, but their pictures were being protected because they were either paying money or paying in other ways."

"Sally's series only touched on that," Esme said.

"Because I got her to agree she could only publish fact-based articles." Andrew shifted his gaze between Esme and Troy. "I bet if you asked her, she still has the original articles she wrote, which are intriguing, interesting, and name people like Billy, Brett, and Micky as players in Cathy's game. But she didn't have the proof. In the series she published, she only hints at that, which still pushed the boundaries."

"Is that what my father wanted to talk to you about?" Esme asked.

"Yes. Our meeting was supposed to take place today." Andrew wiped his forehead. "I was a little taken aback, but Sally told him about my book and he wanted to talk with me about it. I assume it was to talk me out of it."

"What book?" Troy asked. "And why would Sally tell him?"

"I honestly don't know. I'm guessing at this point," Andrew said. "My book deal was announced in *Publishers Weekly* about a month ago, but it didn't get much press outside of that, which I'm fine with. It will get enough when we start to market it. I've been considering including some of the original articles."

"Why?" Troy asked.

"I'm working on a similar case, only my client is serving time in prison and she's innocent. I wonder if my silence on what I knew back then only perpetuated a bigger problem."

Troy's heart pounded. "Have you asked her for them?"

Andrew nodded.

"When and did she agree?" Esme asked.

"Three weeks ago. She was reluctant to give them to me, which I thought was strange. She'd wanted me to tell this side of the story years ago, but I've always worried that demonizing three girls who died in a fire would be cruel. However, I'm not sure that's the case."

Troy's mind exploded with a million possibilities, none of them good. However, they were finally leading them someplace. "Andrew, how long are you going to be in town?"

"For as long as you need me to be," Andrew said.

"The second I heard about what happened to Henri, I got a bad feeling deep in the pit of my gut about the fire at my house. That's not a coincidence."

"Someone is trying to silence people," Troy said. "And it all circles back to Brett."

CHAPTER 14

ESME PARKED her SUV in the driveway of Sally's house. She pulled out her cell phone.

Esme: *I'm at Sally's.*

Bubbles immediately appeared. Her heart fluttered. It had been a long time since she had anyone who cared enough to be worried about whether or not she got to her destination safely or not.

Troy: *Be safe. Watch your back. Text me when you leave.*

Esme: *Will do.*

She tucked her phone into her back pocket and double-checked her surroundings as she slipped from behind the steering wheel. Troy hadn't wanted her to come alone, but Sparrow's office was strapped thin, and everyone at the Brotherhood Protectors was either on assignment or somewhere else. Troy asked her to wait until he could come with her, but in the end, they both agreed she needed to perform her job while he took care of his responsibilities. She promised she wouldn't take any unnecessary risks. She constantly checked her rearview mirror, making sure no one was following her, and allowed Troy to track her cell, just in case.

Worst-case scenario and all that.

She rested her hand on the top of her weapon. She didn't always carry, but today she felt the need. It wasn't so much that Troy had started to act like a worried and overprotective boyfriend, but because she could feel the sense of doom lingering over her head. She couldn't shake the bad feeling she'd had ever since she and Troy had spoken to Andrew. Part of her had wished this could be tied back to her mother. That might make things easier in some ways.

The fear hadn't registered. However, it was there, and she knew it was real. She wouldn't take any chances except for what her job required her to do.

Her father had been murdered.

That investigation was now in the hands of Sparrow and her department. However, the fire was all Esme, and because of the medical examiner's findings, arson was all but a given. It was rare for her office to assume anything, but in this case, they would because it was obvious the fire could be used to cover up the forensics of her father's death.

The simple answer to a complicated case.

Esme raised her finger to ring the bell, but the door swung open.

Sally stood there with wide, teary eyes.

"What's wrong?" Esme asked.

"I'm sorry," Sally whispered as she stepped to the side.

"Shit." Esme stared at the wrong end of a Glock. She swallowed as she shifted her gaze from gloved fingers to making eye contact with Brett. "What are you doing here and why do you feel the need to greet me with a gun?" She figured she might as well dive right in. "And will your buddy Billy be joining us anytime soon?" Billy was supposed to be meeting Troy at his office in twenty minutes. Part of the reason they decided to divide and conquer. If Billy didn't show, Troy would reach out, checking in on her progress with Sally. When she didn't respond, he'd check her location and give her ten minutes or so. If she still didn't answer, he'd be calling in the cavalry.

He might even do that quicker, but quietly.

She told herself she'd be okay and all she needed to do was buy some time. She could do that.

"Why don't you come in first." Brett yanked Sally with his free hand. "And hand over your weapon."

Esme grimaced as Brett shoved his gun into Sally's side. "That's not necessary." Esme unhooked her holster and handed it to Brett. The line of defense she had now was her ability to keep Brett talking.

Hopefully, she'd be able to do that until she could pull her phone from her pocket and manage a message to Troy. Asking to use the bathroom as soon as she walked in wasn't a smart idea. She'd give it a few minutes. Survey the scene first and make sure there weren't any other surprises.

"We both know it is," Brett said.

She had been a police officer for five years. Most arson investigators came from the police department or other law enforcement and forensic agencies. She had the added benefit of having been a firefighter as well. She wasn't sure how that was going to help her right now.

A brief moment of feeling as though she were the most incompetent person on the planet filled her soul.

She'd missed so many signs, yet she had focused on every detail. Deep down, she knew she followed every lead. That she had done her job, and even when her gut told her this had nothing to do with her mother, she still sucked it up and went and interviewed Heather.

However, there were still so many missing puzzle pieces. So many square pegs that she had been trying to shove through round holes.

When she'd been a cop, she spent the entire time in a patrol car while she studied to become a fire and arson investigator. She needed her ability to combine those skills now more than ever.

She stepped into the foyer and did a quick scan, noting everything in her sight.

"I don't understand why you're here, with Sally." Esme didn't want to show her hand too soon.

To the right was a small living room with a white sofa and a light-blue chair and matching ottoman. A television hung on the wall across from a big picture window. To the left was a closet. Straight ahead was a short hallway to a U-shaped kitchen where she followed Brett and Sally.

Nothing seemed out of place.

Except Brett didn't belong.

Sally lived alone. She had no boyfriend and since she moved back after attending college in Utah, she didn't socialize much. She reported the news and people occasionally saw her out.

What had happened in high school had changed her, but she was a decent person who never put a spin on a story. Esme always valued that.

Once in the kitchen, Esme took another look around. Off to the left side was a dining room that Sally used as an office and to the right was a family room with a fireplace. She swallowed, staring at five gas cans lined up nice and neat like stockings ready to be hung on Christmas.

"Sally and I are old friends," Brett said. "And I have to admit I was a little surprised to hear you were stopping by." Brett casually took a seat on the rocking chair next to the fireplace. He ran his hand over one of the nozzles. "I thought you had been taken care of last night, but I guess not."

"So, you admit to starting the fire at Paradise Ranch." Esme stood between the kitchen and the family room, adjusting her shirt, pulling it down over her pockets, covering her phone.

Sally stood to her left, closer to the sliding doors that went to the backyard.

Esme noted they were barricaded.

Shit.

"I did no such thing." Brett made a tsk-tsk noise. "However, I have sources and they told me that there was a fire and you and that handsome boyfriend of yours were trapped inside. That sounds horrifying. You must have been so scared." Brett actually smiled.

Jerk.

"Let's cut the bullshit, shall we." Esme leaned against the counter. "We both know you had something to do with the fire at Paradise Ranch." She pointed to the gas cans. "What do you plan on doing here?"

"Nothing," Brett said. "Except lock the doors, keeping you girls safely tucked inside."

"Are you trying to tell me you believe that just because you don't start the fire, you honestly think you have no culpability?" Esme asked.

"Something like that." Brett nodded.

Esme turned her attention to Sally. "Has he been holding you hostage?"

"Yes," Sally said.

"She can say that all she wants, but this time, the person who is responsible for everything will make sure neither one of you lives to tell any story." Brett rolled up his sleeve and checked his watch.

The first hint of irritation.

In her mind, Esme replayed the footage of the fire at Paradise Ranch. Specifically, the fire pattern and how it pulled away from the building. Going on the idea Billy had been the one who did that and the fact he was supposed to be at Troy's office right now, this could give Esme and Sally some time.

"Maybe we don't live to tell it to the world, but let's tell it to each other." Esme took Sally's hand and squeezed. "I'll start by informing you that we know Billy started the fire. We know that both you and Billy were there. We saw both your cars leaving. I also know you ran me off the road. Not to mention you were seen having a little chat with Billy at the casino, so why don't you tell me what the hell is going on and why do you want me dead?"

"I didn't, but you started poking your nose in where it didn't belong," Brett said. "Billy warned me that you were the best fire investigator out there and you wouldn't leave any stone unturned, but I never expected it to go this deep."

"He didn't think the past would be brought up," Sally, who had been quiet, said. "Which is what he's been trying to keep buried."

"So far, I've been successful and it's going to stay that way." Brett let out a long breath. "All the players are being exterminated and there will be no one left to spill the beans."

"I need to be enlightened." What Esme needed more was an opportunity to text Troy. Just one word and then all hell could break loose. "I have limited information. What exactly don't you want to come out, besides that you killed my father?"

"He died in a fire," Brett said. "That I didn't start."

"That's not what killed him." She inched a little closer and pointed to his gun. "The autopsy came back and he was shot."

Brett drew his lips into a tight line as he jumped to his feet. "You're lying."

"My father's case has been officially ruled a murder. Now, why don't you tell me why he was tangled up in whatever past you were trying to bury." She stiffened and prepared herself for a boatload of lies, but prayed for the truth.

"You can blame that on your ex-boyfriend," Brett mumbled. He waved his gun at both Esme and Sally. "Sit down on the sofa and don't try anything."

Esme curled her fingers around Sally's forearm and guided her across the room. She kept her eyes on Brett who had his cell in one hand and the gun in the other. He turned his back and that was her chance.

As she sat down, she pulled out her phone and texted Troy one word: *help.* And then deleted the text after making sure it went through, just in case Brett found the cell. She shoved it in her back pocket before sitting down.

Sally glanced at her with wide eyes.

"What did Billy do?" Esme asked, wanting to keep Brett talking.

"He thought he could cut a deal with your dad to get his job back and bring me down." Brett turned. His dark eyes hardened with pure evil. "He and Micky had the grand plan where they thought they could atone for the sins of the past by tossing me under the bus with their proof that I started the fire at the Smith house."

A wave of dizziness washed over Esme's system. There were so many answers she wanted. The list of questions was a couple of pages long and spanned sixteen years. Her brain quickly categorized them and even though she wanted to continue with those pertaining only to her father's death, she knew that wasn't where she needed to go right now.

"Why did you do that?" she asked. "What did those girls ever do to you?"

Brett glared. "I've had enough of this conversation." He pulled out his cell. "Sit there and be quiet." He tapped the screen and pushed it against his ear. "Where the hell are you? If you're not here in ten minutes, there will be hell to pay and you won't like the outcome."

"What's going on?" Esme asked.

Brett lunged toward her, smacking her cheek with the butt of his weapon.

Her head exploded with pain. Her teeth rattled. She grabbed the side of her face and groaned.

"Shut the fuck up," Brett said. "Or I'll render you both unconscious."

It was time to take a few minutes to think and regroup.

TROY FOLDED his arms and sat on the edge of his desk. "Why do you think he wants you here?"

"I have no idea," Sparrow said. She had made herself comfortable in one of the chairs by his desk. She looked pretty formidable in her uniform. "But he said it was imperative and would shed light on the case."

"I hope so." Troy glanced at his watch. "I don't like that Esme went to Sally's alone."

"She'll get a hold of us if she needs us."

Troy sucked in a breath as Billy stepped into his office carrying a thick folder. He had dark circles under his eyes. He wore a black T-shirt and black jeans.

Not a good look, considering that's what the culprit who tried to burn down his stable wore. Troy dropped his hands to his sides and clenched his fists.

"Thank you both for meeting with me." Billy stopped two paces inside the office.

"I called you," Troy corrected. "But you did ask for Sparrow to be present, so why don't we forget about the pleasantries and get down to business."

Billy plopped down in the other chair, ran his free hand through his hair, and sighed. "Before I begin, I just learned that Micky didn't make it." A tear ran down Billy's cheek. "This wasn't supposed to happen."

"I'm sorry about that." Troy wanted to put his fist through a wall. "I need some questions answered," Troy said. "Did you know that Fire Chief Henri Jade had the paperwork to fire you, but didn't?"

"Yes," Billy said.

"Why didn't we find the same for Micky?" Troy asked.

"Micky didn't have the same problems that I did, so he wasn't going to get canned. Henri would have approved his reinstatement. I had negotiated with Henri so he wouldn't go through with firing me and Micky and I would stay suspended until we helped bring down Brett." Billy leaned forward and placed a file on the desk.

"And what are we negotiating, exactly?" Sparrow asked.

Billy flipped open the file and pulled out a piece of paper. He breathed deeply and glanced between Troy and Esme. "He promised me he was going to take this to Jim and then to the FBI or whoever. I need to know you're going to honor this." He handed it to Sparrow.

Troy stood and waltzed around the desk, standing behind Sparrow so he could read the document.

Immunity for testimony.

Troy paused reading. "Why or how did all this come about? It can't be just because you got suspended and were about to be fired."

"You're right," Billy said. "It started when Brett got wind of Andrew's book and he showed up here threatening that we needed to make sure we put an end to it." Billy held Troy's gaze. "Brett has the tapes. He also has video of us sneaking around the Smith house. He told us he'd release it, opening up a can of worms that we didn't want out there. So, we went to Henri for help."

"Sparrow, do you have the authority to honor that?" Troy tapped the page. Something rattled his gut. He couldn't place his finger on what bothered him, but for now, he'd play along.

"I can put in a good word," she said. "But I can't make that promise."

"I need someone to swear to me that I won't go to jail." Billy glanced around. "Where's Esme? Is she somewhere else in the office?"

"Why are you concerned about where she is?" Troy narrowed his stare.

"Because I would think she'd want to hear this. Is she listening in?" Billy glanced to the ceiling.

Troy contemplated on whether or not he should be honest about Esme's whereabouts. Telling Billy could give Troy some insight based on Billy's reaction. But it could also put her at risk. However, if the tables were turned, he'd expect her to tip the table.

"She went to Sally's," Troy said.

Billy's eyes went wide. "No. That's not good." Billy shook his head. He jumped to his feet and paced.

"Why. What's going on at Sally's?" Sparrow asked.

"Fuck it. If I go to jail, at least no one else will die." Billy paused, closed his eyes, and planted his hands on his hips. "I'm supposed to meet Brett there in a half hour."

"Start talking." Troy wanted to reach out and strangle Billy, but that wouldn't help. He needed to remain calm and focused.

"Sixteen years ago, Cathy Smith and her two best friends taped me, Micky, and Brett having sex with them, but it wasn't your typical sex tape. It wasn't like what she did with Andrew. Or a couple other guys whom she blackmailed into doing things for her and if they didn't, she uploaded the images to embarrass them. She did that to prove to us she'd do it."

"Get to the point." Sparrow stood and rested her hand on the butt of her gun.

"Cathy liked to role-play and one of them was a rape scene." Billy dropped his chin to his chest. "We didn't know she taped us until she threatened to tell everyone we assaulted her." He lifted his gaze. "I was eighteen years old and terrified. She could have sent us all to jail."

"So, instead, you killed her in a fire," Troy said.

"No. I didn't do that. Neither did Micky. That was all Brett." Billy raised his finger. "But he made sure that if Andrew didn't take the fall, it would be Micky and me. The only person that could identify him had been Sally, but he got lucky when the video from the party of Sally drinking came out and questioned her credibility. And the fact that his parents said they had the sports car that night made it so there was no way it could have been Brett, making Andrew's lawyer look like he was grasping at straws."

"But it was you who set my stable on fire this morning, wasn't it?" Troy asked.

"I did my best to make sure that fire would flame out. I also purposely didn't take out the security camera," Billy said. "Not that I wanted to get caught, but I didn't want anyone else to get hurt."

"What happened in the fire that ended up taking Micky's life?" Sparrow said.

Billy inhaled sharply. "I don't know if you got the medical examiner report back yet or not, but that fire didn't kill Henri."

"We know," Troy said. "So, who did?"

"I can't be sure since I wasn't there, but I'm guessing Brett did," Billy said. "I got a text to meet

Brett at the condemned building. I didn't know that Micky was told to meet him there a half hour before me."

"So, you didn't go in at the same time," Sparrow said.

"No." Billy shook his head. "I tried to save him. I really did. I saw him in a window on the second floor. The stairs were burned out and I couldn't find another way to the second floor. If I didn't get out when I did, I would have perished too."

"So, how do you know that Henri was shot?" Sparrow asked.

"Micky texted me and told me that Brett lost his shit and shot the fire chief point-blank." Billy swiped at his eyes. "I hauled ass to that building. But the worst part and why I panicked was Brett used my gun."

"Jesus," Troy said. His phone, which was on his desk, buzzed. He snagged it, tapping the screen.

Esme: *Help.*

"Fuck. We have to roll," he said.

"What's wrong?" Sparrow asked.

"Esme needs us." He held up his cell. "What the hell does Brett have planned for Sally?"

"You really have to ask?" Billy turned and took two steps to the door.

"Where the fuck do you think you're going?" Sparrow leaped in front of him, shoving him backward.

"I'm sure as hell not going to sit here and do nothing while he tries to kill two more people, especially when one of them is someone I care—"

"Fuck off," Troy said. "You don't get to care about Esme anymore. I do." Troy inched closer and poked Billy in the chest. "I appreciate you coming forward with all this information, but don't you dare even utter her name."

"Fine. But use me to save her and Sally." Billy raised his hands. "Brett is expecting me. He'll want me to start the fire. He's been thinking he can either pin them on me or the Colorado Firestarter's followers. So, let me go and play my role so you can come in and be the hero." Billy pointed to the piece of paper on Troy's desk. "Just please, I beg of you to try to honor that as much as possible. I know I've totally fucked up and my career is over. I accept that. I will do whatever you need me to."

Troy stole a glance in Sparrow's direction. She had the same *I don't believe this bullshit, but we've got no choice,* look on her face that his instincts screamed.

"It's not my call, but you do exactly what Troy and his brothers and I tell you to do, and you have my word that I will speak on your behalf."

"I'll consider it if things go in our favor," Troy said. "I need to call my brothers. We can work on a plan while we drive."

CHAPTER 15

ESME TWISTED HER WRISTS, but there was no breaking free from her restraints. "Are you okay?" she whispered.

"Yeah," Sally said. "I worried when Andrew's book announcement came out, but they purposely didn't make a big deal about the content."

"How bad is Brett going to look in that book? I mean what are your articles like?"

"Well, Andrew has to be careful of slander, so we don't come out and accuse anyone of anything. It's all investigative, but I stand by my research. And I have sources—friends from our past who are willing to go on record that Cathy manipulated a lot of boys from our class in sexual ways and threatened to use that against them. I've always thought that was the key to finding out who started the fire that killed Cathy and her friends."

"Shut up," Brett said as he stomped back into the dining room. "If your ex-boyfriend doesn't show up soon, we're going to have to consider going to plan B and instead of a fire being your demise, we'll have a murder-suicide." He slammed a hard drive down on the table.

"What's that?"

"A recording of Billy and Cathy, only Cathy doesn't look like she's into it. As a matter of fact, the police would probably call it rape."

Esme's throat tightened. "What does that have to do with Sally and me?"

Brett laughed. "I love how you try not to act shocked by what I just informed you about."

"I'm with Esme. I don't know what that has to do with the two of us," Sally said.

"It would be humiliating for Esme since she was dating him at the time and did so for nearly two more years." Brett tapped his weapon against Esme's temple. "But also on this drive is footage of the night of the fire where Sally here had too much to drink, stumbled down to the pool deck, and tried to make out with me where I politely told her no."

"That's bullshit. It never happened," Sally said.

"Are you sure?" Brett leaned forward and kissed her cheek.

She jerked.

"Because I remember it like it was yesterday. It's

the same footage that was used at the trial to show you drinking and smoking a little weed." Brett raised his thumb and index finger to his lips. "That helped prove your judgment couldn't be trusted."

"I still don't understand why any of that matters," Esme said.

"Oh. It gets better. Thanks to a little video rendering, we can see pretty clearly that it was Sally who set the fire sixteen years ago." Brett slapped a piece of paper on the table. "And thanks to this note that Sally will leave behind, it explains how she had to kill Esme when she found this hard drive that her father had in his possession which is what got him killed and it will put this entire ugly mess behind us all."

"You have lost your fucking marbles if you think that story is going to fly," Esme said. Her heart hammered in her chest. The story didn't make any sense. No one would believe it. It was so ridiculously outrageous, but it wouldn't matter. If Troy didn't show up soon, she was dead. She could tell that by the look on Brett's face.

"The best part is this is the gun that killed your father." Brett's phone dinged. He pulled it from his pocket. "Or maybe we go back to plan A." He snagged the paper and turned on his heel, heading toward the front door. "It's about fucking time."

"Sorry. I got called into the fire chief's office. He's a piece of work," Billy said.

Esme's heart dropped to the pit of her stomach.

"What did he want? Did he ask about the fire this morning?" Brett asked.

"He didn't say a word about it." Billy appeared in the dining room. He made eye contact, but quickly shifted his gaze. "Why did you tie them up? If they have rope burns on their wrists, that will give the medical examiner and the fire chief a reason to keep an investigation open."

"Well, well, well. Look at you leaving your conscience at the door. What happened between this morning and now?" Brett asked.

"I'm tired of this. I want it to be over. For good. Period," Billy said.

"We'll untie them when it's time to leave and we're sure they can't get out." Brett waved his gun around casually.

"Okay. But those aren't going to work." He pointed to the gas cans. "Even a bad investigator will know immediately that it was arson and if I go down, you're coming with me."

"You're in no position to negotiate with me," Brett said.

"I'm not. I'm simply stating a fact." Billy let out a long breath.

"All right. But if we don't use an accelerant, how do you expect this place to go up in flames?" Brett arched a brow.

Billy scratched the side of his face. "An electrical fire starting in the kitchen should do the trick. Done right, it will go right through the walls and this place will go up like kindling."

Esme did her best to keep her thoughts from showing up on her face. No one started an electrical fire. One could make a fire look like an accident, but that required walking away and letting the fire do its job. Leaving two people inside to perish added a different element. They were going to have to make sure they couldn't get out. That meant possibly knocking them unconscious, or worse.

But it was Billy's words that didn't sit right with Esme.

Electrical fires weren't started. At least not how Billy was describing it.

"Well, you better get to work," Brett said. "I need to get the hell out of this town. I'm supposed to fly back out of this country in two days. I need to make sure that happens."

"I'm going to need my tool kit from my truck," Billy said. "Why don't you get it while I prepare the appliances."

"Like hell. I'm not your errand boy," Brett scoffed.

"Fine. But we're wasting time." Billy turned on his heel and took two steps.

"Whatever. I'll go." Brett put up his hand. "But let's hurry the fuck up."

Esme wiggled and twisted in her chair. Her nostrils flared. The sound of the door clicking closed sent a shiver down her spine. "When I get out of these restraints, I'm going to kick your ass."

"I'm sure you will." Billy raced to her side and knelt behind her, tugging at the rope. "I need to you to listen."

"Fuck—"

"Troy and his brothers are outside. They can hear every word," Billy spoke softly and quickly. "Do you want them to take Brett down right now for kidnapping? Because that's all they really have. They don't have enough to nail him for your dad or anything else, all the evidence that I've given them, it's circumstantial at best, except he has my gun."

"What does that have to with—"

"My gun was used to kill your father," Billy said. "But even Andrew said Brett, with a good lawyer, could get him off. It's my word against his and he's got a shit ton of bullcrap on me. We need proof that he set the Smith fire. Or something that will send him away for good."

"He told us what he did," Sally said. "And he has the hard drive with him that has all the sex tapes, including the role-playing ones."

"That isn't going to make me look good," Billy said.

"He says the same one shows me setting the fire, but he admitted to doctoring it," Sally said.

"I'm sure a forensic specialist can easily prove that." Billy rubbed the back of his neck. "Where is the hard drive now?"

"Right there." Esme nodded toward the table.

Billy snagged the small device and shoved it in his back pocket. "We don't have much time," he whispered. "Your boyfriend should storm inside any minute now, but until then, I need to go pretend to know how to start an electrical fire."

"Candles near a junction box or any hot wire," Esme said. "You could also leave appliances on with cloth nearby and pretend to knock us out."

Billy's lips drew in a tight line. He palmed her cheek. "I'm sorry. I wish things were different."

TROY PACED as he listened to the conversation. The second they got confirmation that Esme and Sally were alive and that Brett had been holding them hostage, he wanted to go barreling through the front door.

But he had given the decision to Esme, and she wanted more. She didn't want Brett to spend a year or two in jail, or possibly not go at all. She wanted to go for the jugular, and he honestly didn't blame her.

He tapped his earpiece. "Everyone in place?"

"Falco one on the roof next door," Seth said.

"Falco two in the neighbor's backyard," Heath replied.

"Falco three point five on the north side." Leave it to Trent to be the comic relief.

"Falco five across the street," Marcus said. "Brett just entered the front door."

Troy was the only one who could hear what was happening inside. He sucked in a deep breath. "When I give the command, do not hesitate. Everyone understand?"

All of his brothers grunted a response.

He closed his eyes and focused on the conversation. Hopefully, it wouldn't take Billy too long to get Brett to trip up and confess to everything.

Only, the conversation didn't continue as he thought it would. He sat upright. His heart squeezed. "Fuck," he muttered as a high-pitched noise echoed in his ear. He grabbed his earpiece and tossed it to the floor. Billy had a different agenda, and it was all about making sure the past didn't catch up to him.

ESME GLANCED between Sally and the kitchen.

It was too quiet.

Billy hadn't said a single word since Brett had returned, and it had been five minutes.

Something was wrong.

"What are you doing?" she asked. The silence had become deafening.

"Making sure this looks like an accident," Billy answered.

Desperation bubbled from Esme's toes to the center of her chest. Billy's job was to get Brett to talk. Why wasn't he doing that? What had changed?

The smell of burning fabric filled the air. The fire had started. That wasn't good. It was too soon.

"Brett. Why did you kill my father?" Esme asked.

"What makes you think I did that?" Brett appeared at the doorway.

"Because I told her that," Billy said.

"What the fuck?" Brett raised his weapon. "This is not going to end well for you. You shouldn't be saying shit like that. I have the hard drive. Remember, I could ruin you at any second, and let's not forget what happened to poor Micky."

"Don't you dare ever speak his name," Billy said with real venom spewing from his lips.

Esme wiggled in her chair. She had to get out. Now. Billy should have at least loosened her restraints. Shit.

"Besides, what hard drive are you talking about?" Billy asked.

"The one that proves you helped set fire to Cathy Smith's house. Among other things," Brett said.

"Really? And where is this hard drive?" Billy asked.

"It's right there." Brett pointed to the dining room table. "What the hell?" He raced into the room and patted down the top as if the device would miraculously appear. "What did you do with it?"

"All that hard drive does is prove that you and Cathy were predators, and it's going to perish in this fire," Billy said as he dropped a candle to the floor. Fire ignited around his feet, but it didn't catch onto his clothes. "Fire retardant." He smiled.

"You can't destroy that," Esme said. "I'll tell Troy." Her pulse raced. Flames were everywhere. Smoke filled her lungs.

"That's going to be kind of hard," Billy said. "This place will go up too quickly and in the chaos I will escape."

"You won't get away with this." Brett lunged toward Billy, but Billy dodged to the right, and Brett ran into the wall, falling to the ground, into the fire. He rolled to his right, then to his left.

The front door flew open, and Troy jumped between her and Billy. "Don't move, Billy."

The back door burst open, and Heath tackled Brett, successfully putting out the flames that had clung to Brett's clothing.

The rest of the Falco brothers came barreling into the house, weapons at the ready. Sirens sang in the background.

It was Marcus who disarmed Billy.

A lot of swearing was tossed around between Billy, Brett, and three of the Falco brothers while Trent helped untie Sally and removed her from the house, ensuring her safety.

Marcus snagged the hard drive from Billy.

Sparrow entered the house and took the drive, placing it in an evidence bag. She guided Billy out the door.

"Hey there," Troy said softly, removing the restraints from around Esme's wrists, lifting her into his arms and racing out the door. "I'm so sorry. I had no idea Billy would try to pull a fast one like that."

"He might not have killed my dad, but he's guilty as sin," she said. "Give me five minutes alone with him."

Troy set her feet on the ground as the fire trucks arrived and first responders jumped into action.

"Are you okay?" Troy asked.

She shook from the inside out. "Yes. No. I don't know. So much has happened and I don't know how to process this. Billy cared more about making sure his part in the Smith fire didn't come out than protecting me. I don't know how he thought he would get away with this or where he thought he was going to go after he escaped the fire."

"He wouldn't have gone anywhere," Troy said. "I'm so sorry." He cupped her face. "He played us all. But it's over. We have him and Brett. You're safe."

Esme wrapped her arms around Troy's shoulders and rested her head on his chest. For the first time since her father died, grief took over. Her knees gave way and Troy lifted her into his arms, carrying her toward his SUV.

"Put me down," she whispered.

"Sure thing." He set her in the back seat of his vehicle. He took her chin with his thumb and forefinger. "It's time for you to rest. I'm taking you back to Paradise Ranch. You're taking at least a week off of work."

"No. I need to—"

He hushed her with a kiss.

"You haven't even planned your father's funeral yet. I'm calling George and you're not going to fight me or anyone else on this. Got it?"

She sucked in a deep breath and let it out slowly. "Okay," she managed. "Thank you."

"You're welcome."

"And Troy," she said.

"Yes?"

Her heart swelled with more emotion than she knew what to do with. "My father would approve."

Troy smiled. "Is that your way of saying you and me have turned into a relationship of sorts?"

"Don't let it go to your head."

"Oh. It has." He brushed his lips over her mouth. "For the record, I care for you in the long-haul kind of way." He tucked her into the back seat and closed the door.

She tilted her head, looked through the sunroof, and stared at the sky. "Daddy, I found a man who will fight for me no matter what."

CHAPTER 16

A week later...

TROY LEANED against the barn door and stared at the most beautiful woman in the world. He couldn't imagine what his life would be like without her in it. He'd spent the last few years working on getting his brothers all in one place, and now that they were settled in at Paradise Ranch, he realized he wanted something more.

And he wanted it with Esme.

She blinked her eyes open and stretched. "How long have you been standing there staring at me?"

"About ten minutes." He inched closer, setting a cup of coffee on the nightstand before climbing back onto the bed and pulling her close. "Marcus is making pancakes for breakfast."

"I'm going to get fat hanging out with you and your brothers."

He laughed. "Are you still planning on going back to work on Monday? Because you could take more time if you need it."

"No. I'm ready." She leaned in and kissed him hard. "I hear congratulations are in order."

"Wow. That news traveled fast, considering I haven't officially accepted the offer."

"Why would you turn down being fire chief? You're really good at it."

"Thank you," he said. "I'll accept it on one condition."

She tilted her head. "What's that?"

"You don't get too wigged out when I tell you that I'm falling madly in love with you."

Her lips parted, and she gasped.

"I know. It's fast. And we've both been through a lot, but I've been waiting my entire life for someone like you."

She palmed his cheek. "Before I commit, I think we need to break out Trent's Ouija board and ask my dad how he feels about all this."

Troy took her hand and kissed the back of it. "You've been spending too much time with my twin."

"I adore all your brothers."

"Hopefully not as much as you like me."

She smiled. "I'm kind of head over heels for you."

"As in you might be in love with me, or are you still testing the waters?"

"You are so cute when you're insecure," she said. "But I'm ready to jump in with both feet and say without a shadow of a doubt that I love you."

Troy pulled her into his arms and kissed her sweet lips. As a child, his family hadn't been what he needed or wanted. But now, he'd found the kind of family and home he'd been searching for his entire life. He had his brothers—Team Falco forever.

And he had Esme. A woman who not only would he always fight for, but she would do the same for him.

He'd found paradise.

Team Falco
Fighting for Esme - Jen Talty
Fighting for Charli - Leanne Tyler
Fighting for Tessa - Stacey Wilk
Fighting for Kora - Deanna L. Rowley
Fighting for Fiona - Kris Norris

Thank you for taking the time to read *Fighting for Esme*. Please feel free to leave an honest review! Grab a glass of vino, kick back, relax, and let the romance roll in…

Sign up for my Newsletter (https://dl.bookfunnel.-com/82gm8b9k4y) where I often give away free books before publication.

. . .

Join my private Facebook group (https://www.facebook.com/groups/191706547909047/) where I post exclusive excerpts and discuss all things murder and love!

FIGHTING FOR CHARLI

TEAM FALCO BOOK 2

LEANNE TYLER

FIGHTING for CHARLI

BROTHERHOOD PROTECTORS

Colorado

TEAM FALCO

FOOL'S GOLD

LEANNE TYLER

PROLOGUE

"Mayday. Mayday. Mayday."

"This is helicopter 4-3-5-Marcus Falco out of Fools Gold, Colorado. We're headed north northeast to Greeley and experiencing mechanical difficulties. I have three passengers on board, and one of the passengers is in distress. I suspect a cardiac event."

"We're landing North of Denver at latitude 40.039545 and longitude 104.926453. Please send an air ambulance for transport to North Colorado Medical Center in Greeley. Over."

Static came over the line as his chopper blades slowed and smoke clouded the front shield.

No response came over the line. He glanced over at one of his passengers, Charli Jackson, sitting in the co-pilot's seat. She was watching him closely worry in her blue eyes as she bit her bottom lip.

"Mayday. Mayday. Mayday."

"This is 5-Marcus Falco. We're going down now. Do you read me?"

"Marcus!" Charli screamed.

"Charli!" Melanie Jackson called from the backseat. "Oh my God, Gran!"

Fighting for Charli - Leanne Tyler

ALSO BY JEN TALTY

INVESTIGATE WITH ME

SAIL WITH ME

FLY WITH ME

Club Temptation

SWEET TEMPTATION

The Monroes

COLOR ME YOURS

COLOR ME SMART

COLOR ME FREE

COLOR ME LUCKY

COLOR ME ICE

It's all in the Whiskey

JOHNNIE WALKER

GEORGIA MOON

JACK DANIELS

JIM BEAM

WHISKEY SOUR

WHISKEY COBBLER

WHISKEY SMASH

Search and Rescue

The Men of Thief Lake

REKINDLED

DESTINY'S DREAM

Federal Investigators

JANE DOE'S RETURN

THE BUTTERFLY MURDERS

The Aegis Network

THE LIGHTHOUSE

HER LAST HOPE

THE LAST FLIGHT

THE RETURN HOME

THE MATRIARCH

The Collective Order

THE LOST SISTER

THE LOST SOLDIER

THE LOST SOUL

THE LOST CONNECTION

A Spin-Off Series: Witches Academy Series

THE NEW ORDER

Cove's Blind Date Blows Up

My Everyday Hero – Ledger

Tempting Tavor

Needing Neor

Holiday Romances

A CHRISTMAS GETAWAY

ALASKAN CHRISTMAS

WHISPERS

CHRISTMAS IN THE SAND

CHRISTMAS IN JULY

Heroes & Heroines on the Field

TAKING A RISK

TEE TIME

A New Dawn

THE BLIND DATE

SPRING FLING

SUMMERS GONE

WINTER WEDDING

ABOUT JEN TALTY

Jen Talty is the *USA Today* Bestselling Author of Contemporary Romance, Romantic Suspense, and Paranormal Romance. In the fall of 2020, her short story was selected and featured in a 1001 Dark Nights Anthology.

Regardless of the genre, her goal is to take you on a ride that will leave you floating under the sun with warmth in your heart. She writes stories about broken heroes and heroines who aren't necessarily looking for romance, but in the end, they find the kind of love books are written about :).

She first started writing while carting her kids to one hockey rink after the other, averaging 170 games per year between 3 kids in 2 countries and 5 states. Her first book, IN TWO WEEKS was originally published in 2007. In 2010 she helped form a publishing company (Cool Gus Publishing) with *NY Times* Bestselling Author Bob Mayer where she ran the technical side of the business through 2016.

Jen is currently enjoying the next phase of her life... the empty nester! She and her husband reside in Jupiter, Florida.

Grab a glass of vino, kick back, relax, and let the romance roll in...

Sign up for my Newsletter (https://dl.bookfunnel.com/82gm8b9k4y) where I often give away free books before publication.

Join my private Facebook group (https://www.facebook.com/groups/191706547909047/) where I post exclusive excerpts and discuss all things murder and love!

Never miss a new release. Follow me on Amazon:amazon.com/author/jentalty

And on Bookbub: bookbub.com/authors/jentalty

BROTHERHOOD PROTECTORS

ORIGINAL SERIES BY ELLE JAMES

ABOUT ELLE JAMES

ELLE JAMES also writing as MYLA JACKSON is a *New York Times* and *USA Today* Bestselling author of books including cowboys, intrigues and paranormal adventures that keep her readers on the edges of their seats. When she's not at her computer, she's traveling, snow skiing, boating, or riding her ATV, dreaming up new stories. Learn more about Elle James at www.ellejames.com

Website | Facebook | Twitter | GoodReads | Newsletter | BookBub | Amazon

Or visit her alter ego Myla Jackson at mylajackson.com
Website | Facebook | Twitter | Newsletter

Follow Me!
www.ellejames.com
ellejamesauthor@gmail.com

Made in the USA
Coppell, TX
01 April 2023

15077949R00154